SIXTEEN STEPS

A TALE OF DELIVERANCE

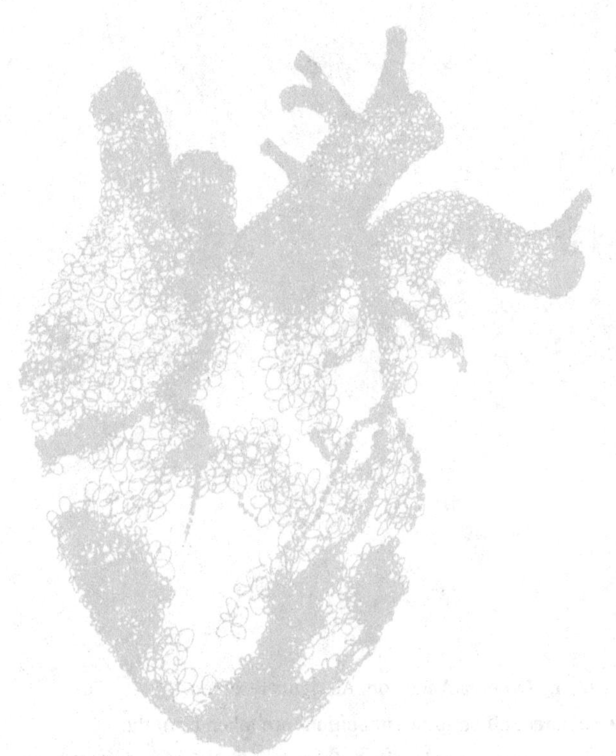

REBECCA ANDERSON

ISBN 978-1-7640624-0-4

To Him, my LORD, my Saviour, my beloved KING:
Your love, Your Justice is transforming; it never stops,
never ends, and never gives up.

To my beloved husband, Grant, and our children, Emily,
Bethany, Jackson, and Phoebe:
my precious blessings and gifts from above
who make life marvellous.

____

*For all the young women unknowingly accused by the adversary,
whose freedom is made possible through His Justice
long before age 36.*

____

Revelation 12:11
And they overcame him by the blood of the Lamb and by the word of their testimony, and they did not love their lives to the death.

Proverbs 27:23-24
Be diligent to know the state of your flocks, and [put your heart] to attend to your herds; for riches are not forever, nor does a crown endure to all generations.

Song of Solomon 2:15
Catch us the foxes, the little foxes that spoil the vines [of love], for our vines have tender grapes.

Foreword

I had the privilege of watching Rebecca Anderson birth *Sixteen Steps: A Tale of Deliverance*, a story that had been carried in her heart for decades. This book reaches into the deepest places of a woman's heart. Even if you do not relate to every step taken by the main character, Jennifer, you will undoubtedly recognize yourself in some of them. At times, Jennifer's journey stirred such profound responses in me that I was caught off guard at what the Holy Spirit was wanting to say to me about my own heart, and His tender love and care for my heart in the process.

Rebecca's intimacy with the Holy Spirit and her love for Jesus overflow beautifully into Jennifer's story, reminding us again and again of His redemption, His deliverance, and His unfailing mercy that is available to everyone who asks. Each page is saturated with the Father's love.

I believe that every woman who reads this book will be touched, healed, and encouraged in ways she did not expect.

Mandy Woodhouse
Author, Coach, Creator, Editor
www.mandywoodhouse.com

Contents

I

Introduction

Jennifer's life unfolds as a timeless parable. A vivid reflection of the sacred journey every daughter of God embarks upon when she chooses to follow Christ Jesus — the KING of kings and LORD of lords. Her story captures the universal heartbeat of a woman's walk with Him — woven with moments of fear, doubt, trials and triumph that echo in the soul of every believer. As Jennifer lays her struggles before the LORD, His transformative, unwavering love, presence, protection and provision shine forth, guiding her to the golden place of repentance and renewal.

Through her encounters with the LORD, Jennifer's faith is stretched, her trust deepened and her spirit is lifted to a higher place. Her experiences serve as a powerful allegory, blending raw human emotion with the boundless grace, mercy and love of God.

This book invites you to journey alongside Jennifer; to see your own heart reflected in her story and to discover the profound lessons that arise when a daughter surrenders to the faithful embrace of her Saviour.

II

Self-justice Systems

In Jennifer's transformative journey, the Holy Spirit guides her through a profound revelation, uncovering a hidden 'self-justice system' within her heart at every step. To her astonishment, she discovers that these inner barriers, previously unknown to her, illuminate a reality she had never before recognised.

Self-justice systems provide temporary relief, serving as quick remedies to soothe a hurting heart. However, these systems deceive; burdening the soul, mind and body with falsehoods that obstruct genuine restoration.

Created by God the Father, the human heart is meant to flourish through His divine justice — anchored in Christ's sacrifice, His Word and His promises. The LORD's compassion, mercy, grace, presence, protection and provision are unmatched.

The enemy seeks to inundate hearts with self-justice systems, numbing and weakening the daughters of God, leaving their hearts barren of Kingdom growth and diminishing the Church's strength and influence.

III

♥

'La-Inyan'

Straight to the Point

I pray that you will enter the hidden richness and depth of your heart as you read. That you allow the things that give you colour, cause your eyes to sparkle and your hair to shine to come to the surface by tilling this ground. I pray your potential is exposed from deep within; to fulfil your purpose and to draw the world around you to Him!

I pray you will experience profound change, growth and mystery through the transfer of your heart. That you arrive at a place of consistent devotion, humility and charity for our beloved LORD.

I pray you will not be disheartened by previous attempts to superficially conquer the metaphorical shadows, short comings and struggles within. I ask for a deep knowing to come upon you, so these things can be uprooted through the renouncing of your own justice system and simply substituting it for His. I pray you recognise your personal justice system for what it is and what it has been within your life... a prison that has kept you in a place of darkness and human fallibility.

I pray you will know and understand that in acknowledging the darkness and making it void, you will be used as a vessel for divine mystery and unfathomable depth. And that you will remember that as the darkness closes, the divine secret place is allowed to come into full bloom, so He receives His full reward.

I pray you will allow the shaking of all personal adversity to bring unwavering devotion to Him. That you would welcome the process that requires exceptional courage and resilience to bring forth an indomitable spirit, divine favour and tangible blessings bestowed by God Himself upon you. I invite you to know that you are a daughter of God, who encapsulates faithfulness, strength and grace, with immense spiritual weight.

I pray you will allow your heart to receive the fulness of His grace so all areas within can be born of light, transferred and resurrected. I pray that as you learn, collect and accumulate His Word and righteousness within your heart, that you would exist only in the overflow of His anointing.

I pray you would be certain; that in opening this door to your royal beauty, you will captivate His heart and the hearts of those around you, to become a beacon of light. A true friend, a passionate, loyal lover of Christ until the very end.

I pray that as you are led by the power of the Spirit and your heart fills with His Justice, you experience what it is like to live fastened to His Glory. Then watch as your whole house binds and unites to His unrestrained truth to repair the foundations within, under the aligning of His hand.

IV

Jennifer's Invitation

As Jennifer entered into her desired place of rest, the LORD interrupted her on a level she had not experienced before. He revealed the purpose of her life and the grand scale of what it was to be…

She was with Him. Completely and fully with Him. She knew Him and He knew her perfectly. His power, peace and love were complete in her. Jennifer knew who she was and what she was for the very first time, made in His image. She had complete clarity and every part of her desired to worship and praise Him. In this state of being with Him, she entered into a large gymnasium.

He was at her right-hand side, approximately three meters diagonally from her shoulder. When they walked in, she observed a large glass wall on the opposite side of the door they had entered from. On the outside of this glass wall were ten or so men in black attire, and a large black limousine. These men instantly detested her presence, cursing her from behind the glass. On her side of the glass wall was a wooden bench with a mangled body on it. Jennifer knew the body was human in her spirit, as the LORD had revealed this to her.

There was no one else in the gym besides herself and the LORD with the mangled body. Then, Jennifer started to praise and worship the LORD with everything inside of her; twirling, dancing and clapping with all of her might in front of the mangled body. The presence of Christ remained complete, positioned to her right side in all His fullness. As she worshipped in this way, the mangled body began to grow back. The skeletal system re-aligned. Limb joined limb. Tendons, ligaments and muscles adjoined the skeleton in harmony and unity, how they were created to be. Internal structures were perfected and skin wrapped around the body to form a beautiful, healthy elderly woman. A handsome long sleeve purple dress with small dainty blue flowers clothed the woman who had emerged from the 'mess' that was. Her hair grew back as a glistening silver crown set perfectly upon her head. This woman laid there, lifeless, in all her beauty.

Jennifer continued to worship the LORD with all that was within her in front of the motionless body of the woman. As she persisted, the men in black attire grew increasingly frenzied.

Their hatred for Jennifer grew beyond violent. They bashed the glass wall and yelled at her. However, she could not hear them; she could only see their mouths move. Secure in her position, she had a knowing that they could not get to her, thus she was unrelenting in her praise.

Jennifer knew that the now whole, elderly woman needed to breathe. As Jennifer thought this, the LORD, knowing her thoughts, sent breath into the woman. The woman began to breathe; she was no longer lifeless.

The LORD then told Jennifer to go to the woman and to lift up her head, which now rested on a white pillow. When Jennifer walked toward the head of the woman, the men in black attire began screaming at her with everything they had, from behind the glass wall. They did not want her to go to the head of the woman! Their anger, hatred and violence toward Jennifer and her actions grew stronger as they bashed the glass with their fists using an even greater force. Their protest toward her position became so loud, it was slightly audible on her side of the glass — "STOP, don't do it, stop!"

When Jennifer lifted up the pillow that the woman's head rested upon, she found her old laptop which she had once used to study the human heart. Jennifer awoke. Immediately she heard the clear, audible voice of the LORD:

"I want you to speak words of life into people."

For days and weeks after this engagement with the LORD, Jennifer was in a constant state of intoxication, unable to function as she had previously. She desired only to lay still and reflect on the dream and the words she had so clearly heard over and over again. It was all she could think about or focus on. It was all she desired; to be with Him again in that dream, worshipping in a way she had never experienced before in front of the mangled body, the woman who came back to life. These weeks turned into months, and months into years, and years into a decade. The desire lived, the desire was alive, but the onslaught from the audible words of the men in black attire had taken its toll...

V

♥

Prologue

From 'Jennifer's Invitation' to now, things had changed. Years had passed. She was no longer working in the medical field. Jennifer's children had grown and she had time to ponder in solitude.

The desire within her heart to fulfil her purpose had grown with great vigour, despite life experiences and her wrestling. She was an unwavering woman; even more determined to fulfil the 'invitation' that she had accepted so long ago.

Even though it had been a decade since she heard His audible voice, something deep inside her heart knew that what happened that night was real. Jennifer had pondered His words, day in, day out, and would unknowingly receive a gentle pruning from the dead wood here and there in her life. This caused the desire to fulfil His invitation to grow stronger and deeper; it produced a certainty that she was created for more from somewhere within her being.

Yes, she had been lied to during this time by the men in black attire. Jennifer could now hear them clearly say to her:

"You'll never. You can't. You won't. You'll fail!"

Yet still the 'something' in her being would not go away.

Then, it was as though the LORD flicked a switch to show her what had been taking place in the heavenly realm over the years. She had, in fact, been on trial. Jennifer had been unaware that every word, action and deed — every struggle she had persisted to overcome with tears — had spoken largely as evidence in the Heavenly court.

The accusations of the men in black attire had driven her deeper into the arms of the LORD and had given her the beginnings of a pure, fortified desire to bow to Him alone. This fire within her persisted to burn vigorously and violently to see her invitation fulfilled, even though she sat in a place of darkness, not knowing how to get out.

All the while, He had been working to re-establish divine order in Jennifer's heart, following and gathering evidence in her everyday life. She was willing and determined, but lacked a 'landing' in her heart to bring forth the blessing she longed for.

The Holy Spirit pressed heavily upon her to align with the LORD; to trust Him, just as Abram did, during this ten-year trial: *"Believe, believe"* He would say.

He reminded her often of Genesis 15:6: *"And he believed in the LORD, and he accounted it to him for righteousness."*

This ten-year period was not a mistake or a place of "no-man's land" as the men in black attire had told her on countless occasions. Jennifer was being trained to become the assistant to the ultimate surgeon — Christ Jesus. She would operate with Him whilst He performed open heart surgery on His people. He would now teach her about the specific instruments He required for the surgery, to rejuvenate the spiritual heart of mankind.

But first, Jennifer had to become the opposite of what she was — a woman nursing wounds of the heart. She had to undergo His surgery herself.

It was time and she was ready. No resource or experience would be left untouched. She would leave it all behind, the things that kept her in the dark, just as Abram did.

The LORD reminded her time and time again of Genesis 12:1-3: *"Now the LORD had said to Abram: get out of your country, from your family and from your father's house, to a land that I will show you. I will make you a great nation; I will bless you and make your name great; and you shall be a blessing. I will bless those who bless you, and I will curse him who curses you; and in you all the families of the earth shall be blessed."* However, Jennifer was yet to understand how this applied to her.

Her broken heart was now to be offered to the LORD as a memorial, thus enabling the 'invitation' to be fulfilled. This would promise spoils of war, gifts of the Spirit, His authority and revelation... and a heart that He could build upon and fill.

VI

♥

The Wrestle of Beginning

Luke 1:37 "For with God nothing will be impossible"

Today, Jennifer's day started as usual. One way or another she was going to achieve her plan. A plan that she traditionally trusted in: coffee, breakfast, some time to write out her dreams, some journaling perhaps, some bible reading if time permitted, the cat litter, tidying the house, vacuuming up cat fur, and walking the dog. Conducting the tasks she deemed to be of great importance... but were they?

Jennifer was called by God over ten years ago, and still today she was left wondering why she was not fulfilling her calling. Why? Simply because she liked being in control, organised, structured, comfortable and knowing what was next. Yes, she was called; but what did she do with the calling? She actually put it into a box called: "I'm so happy to have this, I feel so honoured, so privileged, so special..." and simply left it there.

Until now. Until today. You see, Jennifer thought she was living the call of God out in her life, but really, she was playing it safe. Planning, organising what she should do day in, day out, and throwing some journaling in with it, some bible, some helping of others... that was never Gods idea — it was hers. What she thought it was to 'begin' never seemed to eventuate. She struggled and became frustrated with her life as she continued going around and around, stuck in the same cycle. Deep down inside she wondered if she would she ever finish what she thought she had started?

What now? Jennifer wanted to speak words of life into people as she was told to, but how? Her most current dream had shown her she had some unstable footing which needed fixing. How would she fix this? How could she fix anything with her words? God's Word never failed, but she knew her words would if they were not aligned with His.

'Speak; speak, speak, SPEAK!' That was the bold word that ravished her heart. 'SPEAK!' She wanted to 'shama' the LORD — 'listen and do.' However, she was beginning to feel like it was impossible to live a life of 'shama.'

Jennifer knew she had been given an option — to not keep what she had to herself or she would have it taken from her. What did she have? What DID she have? She had an instruction from God, a mantle to fulfil. How? She would wait and see… NO! No, NOT again, NOT AGAIN! She was 46 years old — surely no more waiting; she was half way through her life! She needed to ask Him now:

"Father, I step in through the veil in faith and trust. I cover my life under the testimony of the Blood of Jesus. Father, I am here to repent for what I believe is disobedience to Your instruction to me that night. You spoke audibly to me; *'I want you to speak words of life into people.'* Have I twisted it all into something which I feel is safe? Am I wrong? Am I just going around the mountain again? I am sorry LORD, I am sorry, please forgive me," she took a deep breath in and sighed.

One of the lies from the men in black attire flashed before her eyes in bold font:

"You will never get this right!"

Jennifer was being accused. "Father, in the name of Jesus, I repent and renounce all agreement with 'I will never get this right,' in all forms and manifestations in Jesus name. Father, what do you see? Please tell me!"

"I see you changing nations, changing the lives of those you love. I see you causing peoples limbs to grow back. I see you living so outrageously for Me that no man will be able to stop you." Father God was confident. He placed His hand upon her cheek, so lovingly and gently.

She pressed into His hand upon her cheek and closed her eyes. She could see a website — 'SIXTEEN STEPS.' It was red and white. She looked at it with Him. "Is this mine Father?"

Jennifer paused and reflected upon some words that bubbled up from inside her being:

'SIXTEEN STEPS for your heart and mine.'

"LORD, each avenue looks impossible… I'm not You, I'm me," Jennifer uttered with disappointment.

She stopped talking and looked at Him. Jennifer then looked down, so sadden by her unbelief. *"Look at Me Jenni,"* He said as He gently lifted her chin. *"That's right, you're not Me, but you are like Me. You are hidden in Me therefore all things are possible. All things."*

She took a deep breath, "Forgive me LORD." Jennifer realised she needed to let go and let Him.

She then watched the pages of the life she had planned float away. Jennifer released her strategies, her thoughts, and her ideas into the atmosphere of His presence. They faded away instantly. She breathed deeply as He took her back to her initial plea from 2014:

"Here I am LORD, send me."

The LORD walked toward her book, the one He had written about her, and opened it mid-way. She felt so disappointed. She knew what her life had been and what it had contained. Jennifer knew she was over halfway through her life on earth, and felt she had not yet given Him a result, nor made progress. She felt stuck and not on channel at all.

Jennifer took another deep breath. The LORD looked at the pages and smiled. She watched Him turn another page and smile again as He chuckled. She wondered what He was so happy about. She was so disappointed with herself; how could He be so happy?

The LORD kissed her on the head and laughed *"I'm so proud of you Jenni!"*

He then walked away. Jennifer's book was left open. She could see the pages of her book before her. "May I," she asked an angel. "Those books are for the LORD alone, but you may see this sentence." The angel pointed at the page that the LORD had laughed at, which contained the sentence she could read. It stated:

"Her heart is Yours; it belongs to You."

"Really? That's what He was laughing about? My heart is His; finally!" she shook her head and followed after Him fervently. "LORD, wait! What do I do now?"

"You simply follow Me," He smiled.

"Follow You where, LORD?"

"Everywhere," He replied.

"LORD, where is everywhere?" She did not understand at all.

The LORD waited for Jennifer to catch up and looked at her closely. *"You follow Me wherever I take you and you live like you are not alone. You live for Me from now on. You can; because I have your heart."*

She smiled and shrugged her shoulders, "LORD, how will I know? I want to know!"

The LORD smiled at her and gently added *"You will know Jenni, you will know."* He tucked her hair, one of the most important assets she had, behind her ears and kissed her on the forehead again. *"Haven't you got dinner to prepare?"*

Jennifer looked at the time "Yikes!" time had escaped her.

She wondered in this moment if every circumstance, every event she had lived through, experienced or participated in, had led her here; to the place where her heart was His.

Jennifer wondered why He was so patient with her? To wait and WAIT and wait for someone like her. She wondered… how much He must love her, how much He must adore her in order to wait. Jennifer thought about her ability to wait — she did not have an ability to wait — especially when she was hungry, thirsty or tired. But He did.

He allowed her to go her own way for such a long time, until she knew that all the world had to offer her was never, ever going to be enough. Then the LORD, just like that, picked her up in His loving arms, pulled out the prickles and stood her up, ready for the next chapter of her life. "I am grateful, so very grateful…" she whispered.

"Jenni, I know you are My dear. But dinner?" The LORD prompted her interrupting her thoughts.

"Yes, I'm so glad You know I have a family and their needs need to be met," she smiled, "Thank You LORD, thank YOU!"

Step One: Self-rejection

Rejection of God's image

"Why? Why? WHY?" Jennifer angrily questioned the atmosphere around her as she wept at her kitchen table. "What am I doing wrong? I don't know what is going on anymore," she howled, slamming her hands on the table, before clutching her head in desperation. Jennifer had experienced life, or so she thought! She was not always a Christian, and was once well acquainted with everything that opposed Christ.

"I don't understand? Nothing ever seems to work out for me! If You love me so much, why do I 'hate me' so much? Why did You make me like this?" she bellowed at the ceiling above her, hoping He would hear and give her the reckoning she desired for her soul.

"What is the point? I don't hear You. Do You see me? Do YOU see this Jesus?" she yelled up, as if to pick a quarrel with Him. Jennifer growled at the atmosphere surrounding her in the silent, still room. She aggressively pushed herself away from the table and stood to her feet as the chair violently fell to the ground. "I GIVE UP!!" she screamed! Jennifer took herself outside for some fresh air to escape what felt like a tangible suffocation in the room. Not another word left her mouth to ensure that He knew He was getting the silent treatment.

The Routine Life

The routine life came into play in the afternoon when her children returned from school. Words were required which felt forced and insincere, but she used them anyway. "How was your day? Did you see your friends at lunch time? Did you learn anything today?" Jennifer had trained herself to respond in an almost robotic format, ensuring the 't's were crossed, and 'i's were dotted' in all her conversation, work and tasks. The same robotic procedure continued on throughout the evening as her husband returned from work. She pondered and rationalised things over and over again. "Do they know? How could they not know how unhappy I really am — not with them, but with me? With life? How do they not see? Of course they don't know; I do everything for them almost perfectly."

16

The Road Block

Jennifer had received a promise from God — she wanted the promise — but it never seemed to come to fruition. Every part of her had marvelled when she heard His audible voice that night. She had tried as hard as she could to cause this promise to unfold, but it appeared to remain stagnant.

Jennifer was seeking a new life through relationship with the LORD; but she kept stumbling over the same road block — shrinking back. Fear had a firm grip on her heart, inhibiting the deep desire given to her by the LORD.

'I cannot' was the true plague Jennifer suffered with. She was unable to trust God and knew that without trust nothing would ever change. So, she continued along the path she had always taken, one filled with words that had no real intention behind them. She used the correct Church language — "I'm believing for this, I'm trusting Him for that" — but the truth was, she did not.

She would be the first one to pull on worldly knowledge, researching every sickness and disease; looking for cures, but never seeking Him to that extent or putting her trust in Him the way she did with worldly wisdom. Jennifer reasoned that the worldly wisdom was made by Him, for mankind. In her mind, that was how mankind got what they needed, that was how they were healed.

Everything was always left in her own hands and up to what she deemed reliable and true, even though she sang the exact opposite in Church on Sundays. This looked good, but her words truthfully lacked substance. All because her heart contained the subtle undertone of rejection. Rejection of Him.

She struggled with pride, but at the same time wanted to hide. Jennifer did not enjoy caring for herself or doing her hair, which had always been fine and limp. She felt that her hair seemed to lack the very element it was made from, which made getting ready to go out for any occasion difficult.

These issues had been present in her life for as long as she could remember. No part of her heart was free from their intrusion. Jennifer was afraid of letting go of what she had "proved" in life, and what she knew to be SAFE. What she had tested brought forth results that she knew she could tolerate, even though these results were never what she dreamed her life would be!

Self-rejection was the only way she knew how to live! It was the first law of her justice system, her own personal constitution. From her perspective if she rejected herself, she would then be prepared when others rejected her. It would not hurt at all because she put up walls. These re-runs had played in her mind day and night without rest. And from what she could see, all of this seemed to be of no interest or concern to Him.

That evening, as Jennifer was preparing for bed, she felt an incredible heaviness upon her heart. But she chose to ignore it, and continued on with the same nightly routine, dragging her feet up the staircase. She was tired from 'life' and excited for nothing. Jennifer forfeited all hope as her neck jarred on her pillow and her body ached on her mattress. "Huh, typical," she grunted, acknowledging that she was unable to even find rest or peace in sleep.

Staircase Dream

As she drifted off to sleep the LORD presented her with a challenge — a staircase. Each step contained a specific 'self' she had depended on that needed to be removed to fulfil her purpose. Each step would release her from the entrapments of pride in her life and render the delays useless as she engaged His Justice. Which would free her from the deceptions of insecurity and arrogance that had held her captive for so many decades. Each step would pull her from trades, contracts, agreements and oaths she had unknowingly made with the opposition, through self-righteousness and self-justification, which held her captive to the blood of Abel. A need for **vengeance**. Jennifer's heart had not trusted Christ to give it His Justice for the pain — it had stepped out on its own.

She looked intensely at the staircase He presented to her, noting its white, shiny framework, impenetrable and narrow. Wide enough for only one. Steep, but not so steep that one could not climb it. Jennifer knew it led to a "broad place," she was yet to understand. A place of asking, seeking and knocking. A place of revelation, marvel, authority and rest. Could it be that He... was finally going to give her rest?

Jennifer now had to choose — to either engage with the invitation to climb the staircase or turn back to her current tiresome life. She knelt down to examine the steps nailed upon the strong white framework, to see what they were made of, as logic had always proved to be a good friend.

When she touched the first step, she knew it was made of Victorian Ash wood, the tallest of the trees on earth. She felt its authority to hold her steady during the climb. A glass framework then appeared on each side of the staircase, surrounding her with a boundary unfriendly foe could not cross — unless she gave them permission.

Next, a silver hand rail appeared, sturdy and strong alongside the glass. She then knew that He would provide all that was required for her to succeed in climbing the staircase.

The invitation to climb these stairs now appeared delightful. Despite her grumblings and grouses at Him earlier that day, He had now presented her with a choice. Then, from this divine presentation as she slept, her heart accepted the challenge. She counted the steps before her with her finger. 'Sixteen.' Before she could lift her foot to take the first step, He told her that this was a journey of love. A journey to engage His perfect love and spiritual completeness.

This would bring divine order into her heart. He reminded her of the Hebrew word 'yod-vav,' the hand of the nail, joining the hearts of two people as one. Each step promised new beginnings — a lifetime of engaging with eternity upon the earth — capturing things outside of time as she knew it.

As Jennifer's foot lifted high in participation from the revelation she had just received, she was shown the cost of the staircase: **His** desires being fulfilled, not those of her flesh.

When Jennifer lowered her foot firmly upon the first step she felt a thunder, a shaking. She knew her heart would become what He had created it be — a place that housed the LORD. She would finally become who He called her to be, 'Jennifer — fair and soft.' She would become impartial and just, without desiring an unjust "advantage" through ungodly trade. For the first time in her life, she would respond to His hovering. She would finally be honest with herself and Him. Jennifer would allow His Word and His Justice to cut; to surgically remove the wounding, bruising, callouses and chastisement from her heart, that she had nursed for decades.

The Beginning

Jennifer opened her eyes — it all seemed like a dream. But was it? It was so real; she knew she was on step one!

"What now?" she whispered into the quiet of the night, gazing around the room looking for a response. *"Come and sit,"* she heard from an unknown source which made her heart skip a beat in anticipation, confirming it was Him. For the first time in her life, she recognised His presence and was choosing to follow Him.

She carefully threw back her bed linen, not to disturb her husband, and when her feet touched the floor, hope increased! Jennifer carefully placed her robe around her shoulders and crept down stairs to find a place to be alone — just "the two of them." With each tiptoe she took through the family home to the den, her heart began to flutter with excitement and energy, as if it had taken flight. She received a 'knowing' that what had trapped her over the course of her life was now going to take a direct hit — sixteen times over.

When Jennifer reached the den, she stepped in and quietly closed the door behind her. She wrapped herself in a rug that rested on the arm of the chair, and snuggled down into the chair's cushioning. She took a hold of her pen and the note book that she had written in many times before.

"I'm ready, I'm listening," she whispered into the stillness. The room seemed to shift to another place, a Heavenly place.

Holy Spirit sat right in front of her, on a foot stool. He gently tucked her fine, tangled hair — which was so familiar to Him — behind her ears and He asked *"How are you, Jenni?"*

She was almost at a loss for words as she looked into His eyes, but managed to reply. "Better, now that You're here."

He responded with a smile, *"It's time Jenni. It's time to become all Father God created you to be."*

"I know," she nodded looking down. Jennifer's lip began to quiver and her whole body began to shake. Holy Spirit gently lifted her chin with His finger, as if to open her airway to bring the breath of life.

The Map

"No Jenni, not like this... like **this**," He coached her as He presented a map of her heart in a tangible vision before them.

Her eyes widened in awe and she asked, "What is that?"

"This My dear is a map of your heart. And we are now going to take back the ground that has been occupied by the enemy for the Kingdom," He clarified.

Overwhelmed, she replied. "How? I've never been any good with maps, just ask my husband."

He answered gently, *"That's ok Jenni. I am here to help you; I will not leave you or forsake you, you are not alone. You never have been alone, My dear one, not once. We have always been right here, watching, waiting,"* He explained.

"For what?" she enquired, confused. "What have You been watching and waiting for? And who is 'We'?"

Holy Spirit laughed, *"Well... quite simply Jenni, 'We,' meaning the Father, the Son and I, have been waiting for you to give up, to be willing to surrender your own justice system for a long time. Some of which you were born into, and some of which you created."*

The Self-justice System

"I have a justice system? I don't even think I know what that it is," she remarked.

"Yes, you do, and it opposes His Justice. A justice system is what you use to make things 'right' in your own life, because you don't trust His Justice to do so," He informed her.

Holy Spirit stood to His feet and held out His hand, *"Would you like to begin? The invitation We extended to you ten years ago can only be fulfilled when you love Him with all your heart,"* He said.

Jennifer paused. Then the words "I accept" flowed freely from her mouth as she took hold of His hand and stood to her feet.

The Ignored Dream

Her heart came forward in her chest and Holy Spirit presented an old dream to her that had been unaddressed. Jennifer did not know that dreams were reference points that needed to be attended to in her life.

She saw her parents' house and a crocodile roaming freely up and down the passage. The crocodile always hid from the rest of the family but she knew it was there.

Holy Spirit then took Jennifer to the kitchen where all her family members were present. Jennifer could see a large python coiled in the centre of the kitchen, then as she looked down she saw the crocodile was clamped onto her right wrist.

"Ahhh! Do something Holy Spirit! It has me, help me!" she yelled, panting furiously.

"It's ok Jenni, I am here," Holy Spirit responded. He gently wrapped both His hands around hers. Tears ran from her eyes and in desperation she pleaded to Him, "Won't You please help me, please?!"

"Shh, do not fear, you are safe. Look again Jenni, tell Me what do you see?"

Jennifer wept as she reported back to Him what she saw. "I see the crocodile. It's still on my hand." Holy Spirit then rested His right hand over her heart, and knowledge was unveiled to her.

"The crocodile had free access to my life from childhood and still has a strong grip on me. I don't know what to do! Help me, please!"

"The crocodile has stolen your inheritance. It has stolen love, strength, faith, blessing, direction, wisdom and authority from you. It has caused you to live a life of self-rejection," He elaborated.

Holy Spirit then released the words that commenced the resection of her heart at the root of self-rejection. *"This Jenni is the issue — the ground of your heart is rugged, preventing you from hearing, seeing, understanding and progressing. Because of this, what has been sown by Us has been taken away."*

The Confusion

"I don't understand," she said as she examined her daily routines in her heart and ran them through her mind. "I read my bible every day for considerable amounts of time. I pray daily, I attend Church regularly!" she stated, justifying herself.

"The seeds the LORD has cast over your life fell on ground in your heart that was fallow — not prepared, untilled, so they could not take root and grow, leaving the seed in a superficial place for the crocodile to remove as quickly as it was scattered. Fear of rejection and self-rejection is used by the enemy to cause you to shrink back, and in doing so, he is then able to use the Word of God against you. This cycle of self-rejection occurs because the enemy does not want you to succeed or to know you are made in Our image. The enemy wants the things you do to be limited and not as effective as We have shown you in your dreams. This is how deception works Jenni! The enemy causes you to look at the 'selves' instead of Father God and you enter a slippery slope of despair and hopelessness, locked in

idolatrous cycles. *And if you manage to get up and going, he brings you straight back down,"* Holy Spirit taught her.

"So, what You're saying to me, is that since I was a child, I have been deceived? Lied to by the enemy" she blurted out in frustration. "It would've been nice if someone told me this sooner!" she protested as she screwed up her forehead and shook her head.

Holy Spirit was silent for a moment before gently taking her right hand again. *"Jenni, We tried. Many, many times. We never once gave up. You have been so deceived, My dear, that you just could not see anything but lies. I'm sorry. We're sorry that this has happened Jenni. This is what he does."*

"But if You were there, how did this all happen?" Jennifer pressed Holy Spirit wanting to know how all of this occurred on His 'watch.'

"We were there Jenni. You just never looked for Us… ever," He answered. *"We gave people free will, remember. We cannot choose for you; you must choose Us,"* He reminded her.

The Truth

Holy Spirit proceeded with a crisp clarity in His voice to address her current heart position: *"Jesus said to him, you shall love the Lord your God with all your heart, with all your soul, and with all your mind. This is the first and great commandment. And a second is like it: You shall love your neighbour as yourself. On these two commandments hang all the Law and the Prophets.[1]"*

She looked at Him stunned like she had just had an adhesive dressing ripped from her heart.

"You simply do not love the LORD with all your heart Jenni. Your heart has been worshipping the idols of self and in this specific scenario; self-rejection. You have been paying homage to it, unknowingly doing whatever it required to continue its processes in your life. Therefore, stopping you from loving yourself and others as We do," Holy Spirit revealed to her.

She replied in a sombre tone, as her heart began to undergo the cutting of His Word. "So, without the 'all' for God, I have nothing for myself or others…" acknowledging what His hovering had exposed — her robotic routines and insincere actions.

"I treat others as I treat myself… without… without… without love, His love," she stated, as tears streamed from her eyes. She suddenly wrapped her arms around Holy Spirit without thought or care, now knowing He had exactly what she needed to be healed.

Holy Spirt embraced her and kissed her on the top of her head and said, *"This is why the 'all' is so important to Him Jenni. It's not a matter of having a perfect heart, but a matter of the 'all' belonging to Him and being willing to remove all the 'ungodly rocks' as I hover over them."*

The First Law

They then travelled through a tunnel that appeared to be made of a dark cloud, and arrived at scenarios from her childhood.

"These scenarios Jenni, contain the outworking of one of your first 'laws' that you used to create your own justice system pertaining to self-rejection. These scenes show that it has been fully operational since age three," Holy Spirit explained.

"How did I do this Holy Spirit? Make a 'law' as a child?" she questioned Him, desperate to know how to end the cycle of self-rejection in her life.

He smiled at her, and advised her. *"Dear Jenni, My dear girl, you simply ask Me where it all started, where the switch was 'tripped,' so to speak, in your life."*

"Ok… Holy Spirit, where did self-rejection start in my life?" she awkwardly asked, following His prompt. Again, He placed His hand over her heart, and as He did she began to feel like she was sitting by a warm fire, wrapped in a blanket of love.

The Cap

"Look again Jenni," He requested. She saw and felt a clear plastic cap coming up from her airway, which caused her to gag as it was projected up out of her throat. Holy Spirit swiftly grabbed the cap from the back of her gullet with a long pair of forceps. She was quick to check her throat with her hands, and swallowed to confirm the obstructive caps removal.

"What was that?! Where did it come from?" she asked with a horse-voice.

"That plug has been in your family line for generations in order to stop you knowing that you are made in His image; a child of God. It filters the truth to remove all supporting evidence that you are loved by Us, stopping you from loving yourself. Now the trigger Jenni, that caused this inherited block to manifest, it needs to be dealt with," He stated in a serious tone.

The Bedtime Story

She saw herself as a young child, around the age of three, approaching her dad to read to her before bed as she usually did.

"Daddy," she said, passing him the book.

"Not tonight, Jenni, I'm exhausted," he replied, patting her on the head. She then watched her younger self run to her room, crying with her book in her arms.

After that she saw herself sobbing in her bed as she tried to read the book. The words were tricky and she immediately became cross with her dad and herself.

Her little heart then engaged with the trade that was whispered into her ear. "It must be you then; it's because you're not good enough." Jennifer saw a scaly, crooked demon, with eyes of darkness and teeth like fangs release these words into her young ears. She then noticed that all the colour had drained from her face, causing a greyness to come about.

Adult Jennifer quickly placed her hands over her mouth, "That's it, that's where it began!" as if to inform Holy Spirit of her new discovery.

He smiled at her and agreed, *"It is! Well, done Jenni. It is here a corrupt law was made, and you can see who helped you make it! This law lacks justice, vision and fairness for you and your dad! The only justice system that is truly just is the LORD's."*

"I don't want this corrupt law to continue, Holy Spirit. I want to truly be who He created me to be. That's why I'm here with You now, right?" she confirmed.

The Redemption

"Exactly" He replied. *"Now, re-engage with the scenario and ask Him where He is."*

Jennifer took a deep breath and asked "Jesus where are You?"

She then saw Him sitting right next to her on her bed with her book. *"Don't be angry Jenni,"* He said with a smile as He brushed her messy, wet hair away from her face. *"I'm here to do your bedtime story."*

She smiled and looked at Jesus, but still felt disgruntled with herself and her dad. However, when Jennifer looked closer at Jesus, she began to recognise Him, His form, His voice. Her heart settled. She smiled and reached out to touch His beard, and said, "LORD."

He then took her little hand and led her up the big white staircase, toward her house in Heaven. As Jennifer walked up the staircase with Jesus, she felt something new; a tangible love, peace and beauty surrounding her. When she arrived her eyes scanned the surroundings that seemed to hum and sing of His glory, the Father's glory.

They sat together on a big golden chair surrounded by light and warmth. Jesus then shared with her some of the plans He had for her future. Her smile grew wide. Jennifer knew she was loved, wanted, treasured, and was pleased to be who He had made her to be.

The Wisdom

"'For I, the LORD, love justice; I hate robbery for burnt offering; I will direct their work in truth, and will make with them an everlasting covenant.'[2] God is a God of justice Jenni, and His Justice system is based on love, not only for an individual but for all involved in each and every scenario. A love-based justice system that He knew had the power to rid all wounding, bruising, callouses and chastisement, for those who were willing to trust it. When you depend upon the system Father God has provided for you, there is no 'landing strip' present for these hindrances to develop or for other systems to be initiated. His Justice is true but also has finite value depending on your willingness to exchange your own

'laws' for His Justice," Holy Spirit informed her.

"I see it now! 'Who can understand his errors? Cleanse me from secret faults. Keep back Your servant also from presumptuous sins; let them not have dominion over me. Then I shall be blameless, and I shall be innocent of great transgression. Let the words of my mouth and the meditation of my heart be acceptable in Your sight, O LORD, my strength and my Redeemer.[3]' I must trust Him to give me justice for the pain," she acknowledged.

Holy Spirit gently kissed Jennifer on the top of her head and embraced her. *"That's right Jenni."*

Chapter Two

♥

Step Two: Self-care

Disengagement with Holy Spirit

Jennifer could smell the pleasant aroma of the tilled ground her heart now contained. With her eyes closed she whispered "I trust You," to Holy Spirit. The three small words He had been waiting to hear for many years.

"As your trust increases so will your joy, because His Kingdom will expand inside your heart and continue to minister to your whole being," He responded as He kissed her gently on the forehead.

"I want You to know, I'm all in now, 'boots and all,'" she stated, with a sparkle in her eyes.

"'Come now, and let us reason together, says the LORD, though your sins are like scarlet, they shall be as white as snow; though they are red like crimson, they shall be as wool.[4]*' During this whole process Jenni, we will reason together just like this scripture says. I will teach you, explain things to you, and help you understand why things have happened in a certain way. I will show you the reasons behind your actions and how your body responds in parallel with what is in your heart. Are you ready to go deeper now?"* He queried.

"I am. 'Oh, taste and see that the LORD is good; blessed is the man who trusts in Him!'[5] I have tasted Him now; I really have tasted His goodness and I really know in my heart He is good! I want to know more, and with my heart, just how good He IS! I want to be blessed by trusting," she urged Him with tears of hope welling up in her eyes.

The Changed Map

Then, He presented the map of her heart before them as a screen; but this time it looked different.

"That wasn't there before," she remarked, placing her finger over the area that once contained muddy water.

He smiled, *"That's right Jenni, it's not the same and never will be again. It has been redeemed."*

Holy Spirit circled the next place on the map to be conquered.

"'I, wisdom, dwell with prudence, and find out knowledge and discretion. The fear of the LORD is to hate evil; pride and arrogance and the evil way and the perverse mouth I hate. Counsel is mine, and sound wisdom; I am understanding, I have strength.[6]*' Do you understand what this means Jenni?"* He asked her softly. She exhaled deeply, and sighed, "I'm not sure, I'm sorry."

"Jenni, no need to be sorry. I am here to teach you; you are here to learn. Sorry is not required in this space, only trust," He reassured her, raising His eyebrows.

The Reasoning

"What We are saying here Jenni, is that We have plans for you — good plans I might add, great plans in fact! To access these plans and get on track with them, a fear of the LORD is required. This means hating the evil in your heart which causes you to house pride, arrogance and insecurities. When you hate the evil in your heart, wisdom pours in, victory comes and Our plans are revealed. You become courageous and strong because you are filled with Us and the Kingdom instead of evil. You can't have it both ways. You can't have evil in your heart and expect the Kingdom to build upon it. We can only build on what is of Us and of His Kingdom. We are only required to bless what is of Us. We keep our Word and our covenant with man. It's like a good marriage Jenni; a marriage is a covenant. The wife keeps her end of the covenant by submitting, listening and following her husband. The husband keeps his end of the covenant by loving his wife, giving his life for her; to protect her, to provide for her. The wife is not fulfilling her end of the covenant when she has other lovers and does not submit to her husband, is she?" He questioned her.

"No, she isn't," Jennifer answered.

"This is why the evil must come out, so that We can pour in Our plans, wisdom, prudence, courage, strength, understanding, and counsel; to give you success for your earthly mission," He added.

"I get it... these steps on the staircase You showed me in the dream, will remove the evil in my heart, and then I will be filled in an immovable way with You, with all of You," she asserted.

"Exactly," He replied with the smile of a proud teacher.

"So, the dream You gave me with the audible instruction ten years ago could not be fulfilled until I hated the evil inside my heart, right? That's what all this is about. You will see to it that the dream and those words which You spoke to me will come to pass then; in the here, in the now — in this land of the living," she clarified, with great anticipation rising up from the small place of trust inside that was filled with His power.

"YES Jenni! We will fulfil Our Word to you. We want you to fulfil your mission, your purpose upon the earth. We want to pour out abundance and blessing upon you

and your family line. It is Our desire and I am here to help you do that," He assured.

The 'Selves'

"You will be required to forsake all other justice systems you have relied on throughout your life, in exchange for His. This includes the systems you created, and those you inherited; they were all formed by evil, and cause you to function with deep wounds, bruises, callouses and chastisement in your heart. These hinderances are what I call the 'selves.'"

"The 'selves' are an entire written text, a corpus, to form a person's very own justice system. The 'selves' are a compartment filled with someone's ideas of rights and wrongs, laws and rulings — which grieve Me! We can never be one with any illegal justice system. We can only be one with the Justice system of Christ Jesus. We will never yield to another. So now you, Jenni, will become a porter and carry the mantle you were designed to carry by filling your heart with His Justice. You will carry the Justice of Christ in your heart; and your soul, mind and body will respond immediately! This is because for the first time in your life, your heart, soul, mind and body will be running on the fuel We designed it to run on — His Justice. You were never designed to run with illegal justice within your heart. Illegal justice is as proficient as diesel in a gasoline motor — the motor just does not work as it was designed to." Holy Spirit stated.

Jennifer's heart desired to release the necessary words to continue the process, but she was unable to due to something rising up from within her that opposed the progress she was making. She forcibly swallowed, as if to push it out of the way, and then she let the words flow that the God-Head had been waiting to hear for many decades. "Will You show me? Show me the evil within my heart. Show me the 'selves' I've been living from… I don't want them anymore. Show me, I want to know Him and His Justice."

Holy Spirit placed His hand upon her cheek and lovingly said, *"I will; but remember, these will all be made void within a moment: self-care, self-annihilation, self-indulgence, self-worship, self-gratification, self-reliance, self-seclusion, self-dependence, self-adoration, self-manipulation, self-dedication, self-conservation, self-congestion, self-service, and self-ruination. You have departed from self-rejection already."*

"That's quite a list, isn't it?" she said disheartened.

"Nothing that cannot be cancelled Jenni. In a heartbeat it will all be gone," He told her.

"This is going to be a marathon not a sprint, isn't it? I was never any good at marathons, I could never finish," she uttered.

"Jenni, you will finish. Even if this is the first time you finish a marathon, you will finish. Remember, I am here engaging with you and I will be here every step of the way. It's not like before, we are a team now, working together," He reminded her.

The Sitting

"Sit with Me Jenni," He said, pointing to the second step they stood on. *"I want to tell you about Me. I am faithful, Beloved. You can tell Me anything. You will not be consumed or overlooked through your honesty, rather you will be led by Me onto a path of repentance. Which will cause the delays in fulfilling your invitation to cease, and bring an acceleration about. Look at the timeline of your life; much of it you have tried to hide from Us and even yourself. All this hiding has done is cause wounds, bruises, callouses and chastisement to rule your life, which, in turn, have caused you to deteriorate. Our goals for you have always been the same — to bless you and love you, to make your name great, so you can be a blessing. Nothing has changed except this, that your new heart position is allowing you to accelerate to your rightful place in His Kingdom, to bless the children of God. This will be your testimony. This, applied with His Blood, will help change the generations. You are bold, you are brave. You are the Beloved. Believe Me when I say I will never leave you nor forsake you, Beloved. I will only ever love you, not beguile you. You can come to Me. I am safe and dependable. I am captivated by your beauty and your song. I am so proud of what you have achieved,"* He explained tapping her gently on the tip of her nose.

Jennifer smiled and replied, "But Holy Spirit, I have only completed the first step."

"Do not be deceived Jenni, that first step seems small, but is big enough to build His Kingdom on. Don't despise the days of small beginnings My love," He prompted.

Silver Car Vision

Holy Spirit then presented her with a vision, *"What do you see Jenni?"*

"I see a little silver car on the highway of life. It has dents; some big, some small. The silver car is smaller than the other cars on the road, even the ones that aren't silver. Smoke blows from its exhaust and it cannot run properly. It can get from A to B but the experiences encountered along the way are uncertain. It has little to no regard for other road users. It's old and in need of significant repair to improve its reliability," she replied.

"Can you see the number plate?" He quizzed her.

She focused again, "I can. It says: 'WKY.' What does that mean, 'WKY'?" she asked.

"WKY, are the twenty third, eleventh and twenty fifth letters of the English alphabet. Numbers 23 and 11 in Hebrew identify states of the heart. 23, the 'kaph-gimel,' represents death and resurrection life. It refers to a lifting up from immorality, stubbornness, grumbling, complaining, wickedness and the idolatry in life. 11, the 'yod-aleph,' represents imperfection, disorder and incompleteness. These are works apart from God — doing what is right in your own eyes, opposing the Word or twisting it, which will ultimately come to collapse. 25, the 'Y,' is the

'kaph-hey' representing blessing. The 'kaph,' is an open palm, to give and cover. The 'hey' is the inspiration, the breath of God — the Holy Spirit, Me! This is the strength and power to go the distance to spread the seed, the Word of God. 25 is also the age that priesthood apprenticeships would begin," He explained.

"These sixteen steps Jenni, will remove the 'WK' by the roots, which hides deep within and has caused your heart, soul, mind and physical body to be dented and to run erratically on the highway of life. You will no longer be a small dented silver car that does not run properly."

The 'Elizabeth'

"You are about to undergo a deep consecration process, which I like to call the 'Elizabeth.' A consecrated heart is what you were created for. The 'Elizabeth,' is the heart becoming so deeply engaged with the God-Head, that it is filled with absolute delight as it depends only upon the Justice of Christ. The 'Elizabeth' heart has no room for its own justice because it is filled to overflowing with God's Word, His promises, abundance, wealth, affluence, opulence and plenitude; the richness of His Kingdom. It is fulfilled by Him in a place of 'sheva' (oath). This heart, is a place of 'Eden,' the garden of the God-Head. This is where the Father, the Son, and I, the Spirit, enjoy living with you in the paradise within, which brings Us great pleasure and delight."

"The 'Elizabeth' heart is not perfect, yet it is beautiful, and completed by the God-Head, because it is willing to receive the Justice of Christ for every pain. It allows no wound, bruise, callous or chastisement to abide, and it is willing to remove every 'WK' I place My finger upon. It is a heart that daily regenerates its strength, yielding to, trusting in and relying solely upon the proven Justice of Christ; never tempted to trust its own. As it is written in John 12:24-26, 'Most assuredly, I say to you, unless a grain of wheat falls into the ground and dies, it remains alone; but if it dies, it produces much grain. He who loves his life will lose it, and he who hates his life in this world will keep it for eternal life. If anyone serves Me, let him follow Me; and where I am, there My servant will be also. If anyone serves Me, him My Father will honor.' The consecrated heart, the 'Elizabeth' heart enjoys 'death' to all self-justifications, insecurities and arrogance. And believes Christ IS Justice and truth," Holy Spirit taught her.

"Holy Spirit, I want this; I want the 'Elizabeth.' I can feel the power and the weight of what You have said to me deep inside." Jennifer then placed her hand over her heart, longing for her heart to be made by Him.

The Second Law

Holy Spirit held out His hand, inviting her to now stand with Him on the second step.

"No great warrior has ever overcome by sitting down have they?" He coached her as He tucked her hair behind her ears to enhance her hearing.

"Self-care is what must be overcome here. What you must understand is the things attached to this have been hidden from you and there will be some discomfort involved. But the reward is great — He is, after all, your very great reward," He reminded her.

With a deep breath, Jennifer replied, "I am prepared to go through some discomfort. I can't go back, I feel as if I know too much already," she stated, knowing confidently that Holy Spirit was (and is) the only One able to direct her around her heart. She knew Holy Spirit was (and is) the One who could lead her to Jesus — the only One who could heal her heart.

Holy Spirit began to teach her. *"Self-care has caused this area to be traded upon by the opposition, in fear of Father God denying you the things you enjoy. Because of this you have only a poor substitute, a limited stringent story for your life which you have placed a sticker upon and called it 'the LORD's plan.' You have protected this plan at all costs and mantled yourself with it. You have been accountable to 'it only,' believing God's plan for your life isn't as good as yours. It has kept you driven and locked into what I call your own perceived '2D' ability to govern and judge the use of your resources, skills, and talents according to the self-care trade agreement. This agreement ensures that gifts from Us are used to worship the enemy, to build his kingdom — not Ours. This has affected your work, relationships and worship; right down to the activities you participate in. This agreement removes flexibility from your life due to its association with fear. Unfortunately, you have become so tightly bound to your own story that it has left you trapped, hence the desire to ensure all your cares were met; and met independently of God, I will add, so you could maintain your idea of freedom. Yes, you have given your life to Christ, attend Church, pray often and read your bible. However, self-care has caused you to lack the ability to reason with God from the void of relationship and fellowship with Me, the Holy Spirit. The depth of this personal justice system is toxic to your heart."*

"What? I think I need to sit down Holy Spirit, I feel as though I'm going to faint," Jennifer said, panting, as things around her seemed to become unsettled.

"No Jenni, not like this, do not engage with what's feeding off of this place. Look at Me. We do this together, you and Me; we are one remember?" He prompted her, placing her right hand in-between His.

"All of this started somewhere Jenni, everything has a beginning and an end — except Us," He stated.

A picture then presented itself in her heart from when she was younger. *"What do you see Jenni?"* He asked.

The Dog Show

With a smile she responded, "I see our family at the dog shows, with our Afghan Hounds. I love those dogs. I now see my mum measuring me up for my dog show outfit, a dress. I love it. It's white, with a navy-blue sash. I feel so beautiful. I can see myself jump out the car with excitement, but then... oh... oh," she suddenly stopped engaging with the vision.

"What do you see Jenni? Keep looking, can you describe what is going on? You're nearly there," He urged her.

"My..." swallowing deeply, she continued, "... my dress, it's a 'poor substitute,' I am ashamed of what I look like, I am embarrassed. I have a 'poor copy' of the original."

"Jenni, who told you that? Can you see them? Please look for the one who told you," He directed her.

She wiped tears from her cheeks and re-engaged with the scenario. "I can't see anyone. No one is talking to me, no one. I'm trying to focus. My goodness, I feel something... it's a breath... it's breathing down my neck," she cried, screwing up her face, and beginning to gnash her teeth.

"I'm going to look toward what's causing the horrible breathing on my neck... I'm turning to it now. I'm going to open my eyes..." Jennifer breathed in and paused; and when her eyes opened, they widened with fear.

"What do you see?" Holy Spirit persisted, waiting for her response.

"It's... it's a demon! Something that looks awful. I can't describe it; it's a lying one though. I recognise it. It's been following me around for a long time. Holy Spirit, what do I do?" she asked beginning to panic.

The Redemption

"Look for Him Jenni, look. Call upon the name of the LORD," He advised her.

Jennifer closed her eyes as she turned to the face the demon once more and released the words as loudly as she could, "Jesus, where are You? I need You! Help me, please Jesus!"

Suddenly, Jennifer felt a hand lift her chin, something had changed. Something big had just happened. With another deep breath and a small measure of peace, she opened her eyes to see who it was or what it was lifting her chin. Then, her whole body relaxed. It was Him before her — JESUS. She closed her eyes again to enjoy the power of His love washing over her heart from the touch of His hand. Jesus smiled at her; He imparted truth into her heart.

"Jenni, did you know yours is an original? There is not another like it. The stitching is good quality because it's handmade." Jennifer pondered this as her child self, looking at her dress again, examining the fabric and stitching on the skirt in her hands. It felt nice, it was comfortable and the stitching did look good. Jennifer smiled. *"What you have is an original Jenni, not just a 'run of the mill.' Come with Me."* He said, as He offered her His right hand to hold. She took hold of His hand and they went up the white staircase together.

Jesus took her to the room in Heaven that contained her book. In which all her days were fashioned, even though she had not yet fulfilled them. He started to turn the pages for her while she watched on in awe. Images flashed up before her eyes. Trust, excitement and joy bubbled up inside of Jennifer.

"This is all for me LORD?" she asked Him to clarify. *"Yes, it is; all of it. Originally written by Us for you,"* He replied. *"Remember Jenni, We know what you love because We put it inside of you. It's important to Me, to all of Us, that you have everything I paid for you to have here, so it can be transferred to the earth,"* He explained.

"Thank You LORD. I have never understood; but now I'm beginning to," she responded, with a rosy smile.

Jesus brushed her cheeks with His thumbs, as He gently held her head between His hands. He then looked deeply into her eyes, *"All for love, Jenni; it was all for love,"* He said.

The Wisdom

"Where did that demon come from Holy Spirit? I felt like it had followed me for a long time?" she enquired.

"That's a good question Jenni. Rejection of relationship with Me and what We have for you was in fact buried in your family line; and although mankind chooses to believe family lines have no effect on their lives, they do. We see them outworking daily. Things that happened decades ago or even hundreds of years ago in your family line, that have not been atoned for under the Blood, give wicked spirits a legal right to 'attach' to the ungodly agreements, trades, contracts and oaths. These ungodly things are what create the wounds, bruises, callouses and chastisements that wicked spirits feed from. They wait for just the right moment to attack like the roaring lion described in 1 Peter 5:8, 'Be sober, be vigilant; because your adversary the devil walks about like a roaring lion, seeking whom he may devour.' That's why you were an easy target. A callous was already there in your heart which you inherited in the womb. The enemy was just waiting for the best time to attack. A callous that turns into a wound is like a double whammy for wicked spirits, because they are harder to heal, which helps secure the longevity of their food source. The better planned their attack is, the more likely their ambush will succeed. Hence, ensuring the prosperity of the wicked things in his kingdom. However, this is not the case for you anymore — you are free. This trade has ended."

"I'm so happy! Thank You," Jennifer replied from an authentic place of gratefulness.

Chapter Three

Step Three: Self-annihilation

Estrangement from the Father

Jennifer's heart ached. A heaviness came upon her that seemed to arise from something so deep within that it laboured her breathing. Everything began to take on a state of slow motion; all she could do was slightly turn her head toward Holy Spirit, because the rest of her felt like it had gone missing.

"Jenni, it's ok. We are doing this together, to bring your heart back to your first love," He said to reassure her.

The Promise

"Jenni, today your ability to build with Me will be returned. Your creative abilities will be reinstated and renewed, and your walls will begin to be repaired and restored." Holy Spirit declared. *"Today you will begin to know you are accepted, attended and protected; guided in all things."*

The slow motion field then seemed to disappear in response to His words.

The Entrapment

Pictures spilled out in Jennifer's heart; much like a jig-saw being tipped out in front of her. From this, she could see that a part of her heart was imprisoned. 'Imprisoned by who?' she wondered.

"Look closer Jenni," Holy Spirit told her. As she drew closer, she understood that she was the one who had chosen to permanently keep this part of her heart in a prison cell. Stunned, Jennifer watched herself rise in this cell, only to reach through the bars with a black marker to cross her name out on the identity plaque wired to the cell door.

Jennifer was distraught. The prison cell door was ajar — unlocked! "Why I am stuck? Unable to move from this dark cell despite there being an exit point. DESPITE there being an exit point!" she yelled desperately under the influence of the spirit of fear. Jennifer quickly realised 'it' occupied this place with her — she had invited 'it' in! She looked back and helplessly saw herself rocking in a sitting position on the cold cell floor with her arms wrapped around her knees, while she sobbed and gnashed her teeth.

"*Jenni, Jenni!*" Holy Spirit called her to draw her attention back to Him, "*Look at Me! You have traded part of your heart, for this cell, this place of weeping and gnashing of teeth. 'But the sons of the kingdom will be cast out into outer darkness. There will be weeping and gnashing of teeth.*[7]*'*"

"How do I get free?!" she cried.

"*You need to invite Him into this place of anger and rage toward self, Jenni. Go back to the vision and call upon Him. 'Nevertheless the solid foundation of God stands, having this seal: 'The LORD knows those who are His, and, let everyone who names the name of Christ depart from iniquity.*[8]*' You must leave this place of iniquity, but I cannot do it for you. You must choose for yourself, you must **want** to leave. I am your Counsel, your Comforter. This is My counsel to you — 'leave this place.' We have given you free will Jenni, you must choose to leave on your own accord,*" Holy Spirit clearly stated.

Jennifer's weeping increased with the realisation that in order to leave this place, she must trust Him even more! She now had to trust that He had something greater — something that would enable her to leave this cell behind, once and for all.

The Changed Map

Holy Spirit then placed His hand over her heart. "*Look at the map Jenni, and tell Me what you see,*" He prompted.

Jennifer was drawn to what she saw: "I see two flickering lights. The light is a reflection upon a clear river in my heart, now existing from what You have taken me through Holy Spirit. The light is a reflection of Jesus!" Jennifer exclaimed, now remembering what He had done for her in the first two steps!

"*That's right Jenni. He will not let you down. It's safe to leave. In leaving this place you are seeing to it that He gets His full reward for His sufferings. This part of your heart, and the parts to follow, will be returned to Him and hidden in the secret place which cannot be shaken. You and your heart, Jenni, are part of His body and He wants all of His body healed by the resurrection power of His Spirit. Just as His physical body was healed and raised from the dead by the Spirit — by Me. Just as we did before Jenni, in the first two steps, we will go back. All you need to do is call upon Him,*" He explained.

The Cell

She began to engage again with the dark, cold cell where there was neither sound nor life. Then suddenly, she broke the silence in the cell and yelled out, "Jesus!... Where are you?" Jennifer called on Him with such force that it felt as if the words released had pierced her stomach. Immediately her jaw relaxed. The grinding of her teeth ceased. "Jesus!" she beckoned Him again! Jennifer then heard a drip, one drop of water. She saw with the eyes of her heart that it was clear living water which had presented somewhere in the prison cell. She could feel it in the darkness. Her breathing became heavier and rapid as the spirit of fear tried to prevent her from engaging with the drop of living water.

Then, without warning, Jennifer let out the ginormous lie that had kept her entrapped for decades. She shouted from the top of her lungs, "I deserve to be **punished**, I deserve to be damned!!" As the words left her mouth, Jennifer could now see Him. He, 'Jesus,' was right next to her, crouching down alongside her. Everything around her seemed to pause as Jesus gently tucked her highly valued, yet sweaty, dirty and matted hair behind her ears and kissed her on the forehead.

"Jenni, My beautiful Jenni, what are you doing here My darling?" He asked ever so gently. Her grimy face looked toward His. Her eyes were filled with pain and desperation.

"I deserve to be punished — damned."

"Do you not know I have paid for your sin?" Jesus gently asked her.

Tears gushed from her eyes, down her cold cheeks. "I do. But don't you see, I'm not good enough! No matter what, I can never be good enough for Him! No matter how hard I try, I am never enough, never acceptable! I must stay here until I am! This is all I deserve!" Jennifer howled, as she exposed the lies that had kept her entrapped in this place of internal agony and grief.

"Good enough for who Jenni?" Jesus questioned her again.

"For Him?" she responded as she wiped her tears on her forearm. Jesus smiled at her, *"Jenni, I am the One who makes you good enough, there is no other requirement. That is all. You have nothing to add or prove My dear."* Her stomach began to swirl as Jesus then sat next to her on the cold, hard floor, and placed His arm around her. *"Jenni, I think it's time we take a look at what brought you here?"*

She nodded her head, knowing that this time she would get out once and for all. Jennifer glanced around her cell, which was now illuminated from engaging with the LORD. She saw everything she had tried to become perfect and acceptable on her own, and could see she had filled the cell from the floor to the ceiling. The only space left was the tiny area she sat on alone, or so she thought, until now.

Jennifer then realised that Jesus was the only One who had ever sat with her in this prison on the cold, hard floor. She now understood He had been there the entire time, but she had chosen to ignore Him. Jesus was there not to offer another presumptuous solution, but the way out. She now knew, He WAS the way out. He did not offer hope deferred, as all her other attempts had before. He **was** her hope. He was not there to cause her to strive further, to enable her to punish herself in a greater measure, to exhaust her or to pressure her; He was there to free her. She breathed deeply in and out and began to compose herself. Yet this time, not by force. Simply from the security provided to her from finally engaging with Jesus who sat next to her. She smiled, but not with the forced smile that had masked the prison within for decades, but with a new soft smile that brought forth a small light.

"Jenni, I want you to look into My eyes," He gently directed her. As Jennifer looked she clearly saw a fire — a refining fire filled with passion, filled with love. Not just any love, an absolute love; THE LOVE.

The Bonfire

Jennifer saw herself as a young teen, enjoying some potato chips at a bonfire event, warming herself by the fire. She was a curvy teen, without a care in the world, and she loved the outdoors.

Jennifer moved her hips to and fro to the music in the background, as she chomped away on the potato chips. Then a man came to warm himself by the fire and stood next to Jennifer. She smiled at him and said "Hi," and then happily continued chomping away.

In that instance, 'that man' let out the words that changed her life. "You know, I don't think anyone has told you yet, but no guy wants to wake up next to a fat b*#@h." Then 'that man' simply walked away.

Jennifer immediately stopped eating the potato chips and threw them into the fire. She stood frozen. The eyes of her heart quickly began scanning through the 'ungodly rock pile' within its walls, looking to confirm if this intel was correct or utterly false. Immediately, Jennifer knew she had to learn as fast as she could what she had to do to lose weight. She didn't want to be alone. Jennifer wanted to marry one day and have children... but how could she if she was fat!

Her heart decided that she had to leave her childish ways behind and change or she was going to be alone!! She vowed to never eat another crumb of potato chips again — clearly there was something wrong with her. Otherwise, why would 'that man' have bothered her with the warning?

In her young, tender heart Jennifer began to inflict internal punishments upon herself and damn herself until the day she would be acceptable to men, no matter what it cost. Her heart raced and she began to search for recompense for the deep wound that had formed within, as a result of her own reasoning. She looked around; 'that man' was right — there was no young man talking to her!!

The Redemption

Holy Spirit interrupted her despair and whispered into her ear, *"Look for Him."* Jennifer frantically turned her head left to see if she could find Him yet she saw no one! Her panic worsened; she was alone! Soon, she turned right and there He was — Jesus.

He smiled at her, *"What's going on?"*

Jennifer took a deep breath and began to let the cause of the pain out. "'That man'... he..." she muttered through tears.

Jesus looked at her with absolute love. *"Come here Jenni,"* He said as He embraced her. She pressed her face against His chest, feeling the scars on His chest press back against her through the fabric of His garment. Jesus then presented Jennifer with His advice that began to change her heart. *"Jenni, don't listen to him."*

Jennifer looked up at Jesus. He had paused the process of the pain and stopped it from taking root before the wound could set into a place of rottenness, slough and malodour. *"'That man' is hurt. He has not yet engaged with My Justice, but he will,"* Jesus informed her.

"So, it's not me?" she quizzed Him to double check. *"No Jenni, it's not you,"* Jesus replied, tapping the tip of her nose.

"You are unique, lovely and admirable. Come with Me, I want to show you something," He said, directing her gaze toward the big white staircase. Jennifer started to imagine what could possibly be at the top of the staircase — Heaven, Jerusalem, the temple, angels, the throne room? Jesus led her up the staircase to a white door in His Heavenly Kingdom. As He started to open the door, she peeked inside to see the area that lay behind it. Her jaw dropped and her facial expression was one of sheer joy, amplified to an unfamiliar scale! When He had opened the door widely before her, waves of light that were full of joy, life, peace and love penetrated every part of her. She looked up at Jesus in awe and wonder at all she saw and felt. He smiled and told her, *"It's your inheritance Jenni — go on, go in, it's yours."*

Jennifer saw her life! In that moment Jesus revealed to Jennifer her future husband in his younger state. She was ecstatic, and instantly in love with him. Jesus laughed, and said to her, *"I knew you'd love him! You'll be just right with him. You'll make a great team you know."* Her heart filled with joy. "Thank You LORD, I look forward to all You have given me, just the way I am."

The Wisdom

Tears of joy gently ran down Jennifer's pink cheeks. The LORD, had set her free! "I'm free, Holy Spirit!"

"You are indeed Jenni! You have received His Justice for the pain. It's wonderful isn't it, there is nothing like it upon the earth," Holy Spirit reminded her.

"I can't believe how I didn't see all of that; the things I was trying to use to heal myself from the outside. It seems so obvious now," she explained to Holy Spirit, feeling enlightened.

"Well, it's because in the exchange you had made, every attempt made by your hand would appear as though it would heal you. That's what you agreed to unknowingly, but each attempt gave false hope with no result. It kept you in

that self-annihilation cycle. You were deceived when you made the trade Jenni; mankind does not know when they are being deceived. If they did, they wouldn't be deceived, would they?" He clarified.

"I guess not," she answered.

He continued. *"External measures are applied by people and seem effective for a time but they are not permanent. The external measures are only successful for the short time they can deceive the eyes of the heart, with the false message that 'all is well.' This false message in turn deceives the soul, the mind and the body. But, over a short time when the "new" external measure fails, and it does fail, the eyes of the heart learn the truth. The eyes of the heart then see the presence of wounds, bruises, callouses and chastisement. This truthful information then feeds through the soul, the mind and the body. The person is then no better off than they were before they tried the "new" external measure. His Justice is the only thing that changes the heart. It is the only thing that heals. His Justice does not apply cycles of remission from the hindrances as external things do; it just heals. It heals once and for all. The wound you had caused the surrounding tissues to be inflamed and tender, which you unknowingly guarded. You avoided putting pressure on it, lying on it, and always ensured the area was kept elevated. Sometimes you attended to this wound several times a day with every external measure you could resource. This is why it only grew worse over the years as all of the external measures caused the wound to deteriorate further, increasing hopelessness. Remember wounds only heal from the inside out."*

"The wound started where and when the pain started. Again, this is the reason the LORD intervened at the exact point in your heart to remove the pain. His intervention then made that part of your heart new, as though there was never a wound or a trade to begin with. Automatically disabling the process that followed: wound infection, redness, odour and inflammation of the surrounding areas. He made it as if the painful experience had never happened. 'Ab initio' — as if it never existed, from the very beginning." He taught her.

"Although you knew Jesus and had given your life to Him, this part of your heart did not know Him as the LORD God. This part of your heart, even though you are His daughter, was outside of Father God's protection and provision. It was placed in what can be only be compared to a "shanty prison." In reality you had no protection and you were left exposed to be an easy target," He added.

"Oh, so why were the words from 'that man' so effective in the first place?" she asked Holy Spirit.

*"Simply because you inherited a calloused heart from conception. All it took was a few short words to trigger the callous that had laid dormant to turn into a wound. A callous heart comes with an inability to see and hear the LORD, it is easily led into trading for justice. In this space of trade, one is not abiding. Even though there is a desire to abide, the heart is unable to. Thus, leading to a 'self.' Depending on the pain and how the person seeks to remove it on their own, it leads to a life of performance works in which people take it upon **themselves** to*

bear good fruit. However, this does not work, as true fruit only comes from abiding in Him — 'I am the vine, you are the branches. He who abides in Me, and I in him, bears much fruit; for without Me you can do nothing.⁹'"

"This indicates that the cycle of self-annihilation is an idolatrous one. It is supported by a stronghold and circumstances often inherited from conception to form a belief system and heart position. These strongholds and cycles of idolatry cannot be broken without the LORD; He is the only deliverer. Acknowledgement, in My view, is the most difficult part for the human heart; but it is the most important as the choice to repent brings that part of one's heart back into the protection of the LORD God. This is where trade cannot occur and vulnerability is never present." He informed her.

"I'm so glad I trusted You enough to see it through the scenario with Jesus, which brought that part of my heart back into our Father's protection and provision, a place of rest. That's just how it was before I was sent here to earth, wasn't it? All of my heart belonged to our Father then, didn't it?" Jennifer quired.

"Yes Jenni, it did. Thus says the LORD: 'Stand in the ways and see, and ask for the old paths, where the good way is, and walk in it; then you will find rest for your souls. But they said, we will not walk in it.[10]' He is the good way. He is rest, but the heart must choose. You have chosen well," Holy Spirit smiled, kissing her on the forehead.

Step Four: Self-indulgence

Ignorance to the presence of Christ

Jennifer felt her gut react from her position on the fourth step and began to feel wobbly and light headed.

Nausea set in and she felt as though she was going to faint. "Holy Spirit, I need to sit down. I can't… I just can't" she said, holding her head in her hands. The swirling felt like it was attached to a vortex, dragging her down. "Oh dear," she cried, grimacing from the discomfort her whole body was now experiencing.

Jennifer took hold of Holy Spirit's arm to stop herself from tumbling backwards. The pain in her stomach began to sharpen. "Augh!" Jennifer yelled as she reached for the silver railing, determined not to collapse.

The Soothing

"*Shhh, Jenni, I'm here, you're safe with Me,*" Holy Spirit reminded her. Jennifer looked at Him momentarily, panting with her nostrils flaring, unable to stand up straight from the pain.

Tears streamed down her face and a blackened trail formed on her checks from old mascara, as if to cross out the ability for her to experience joy. Holy Spirit rested His hand on the top of her head and began to sing over her.

Jennifer started to smile and became mesmerised with His song. As a smile stretched across her face, it cracked the black lines on her cheeks and the tiny black particles started to fall like ash beneath her feet.

Jennifer joined Holy Spirit's song by humming along to the tune He was singing. She quickly became lost in its beauty and released her hand from the silver railing to offer it to Him in worship. She began to see herself as a little girl in a beautiful white dress with a red sash around her waist and a red bow in her hair. She was playing with other children in a meadow, enjoying the flowers and long swishy green grass that brushed against her legs as she ran and played. She picked a flower and breathed in its fragrance; it almost intoxicated her.

Then, all of a sudden, a headache started to develop, interrupting her peace. "Oh no… a migraine!"

"Do not be afraid Jenni. What is causing the migraine cannot stay," He advised her as He stroked her cheek with His thumb.

Jennifer's heart began to offer up a picture as if to present it to her for analysis.

The Black Hole

She started to look deeper into the picture and discovered it was a picture of a hole in her heart that was black, dry and absent of life. She reached out and touched the edge of the hole with the tips of her fingers. As she did, a slight glow formed around its rim and the pain in her head seemed to diminish.

"This is a place of palliation Jenni. A place of death within your heart in which you have refused a cure," Holy Spirit outlined.

Her fingertips instantly pulled back with His explanation and her eyes enlarged from the shock of His words.

Holy Spirit drew her back to the black hole within her heart. It still had the small amount of light around the rim from her touching it. *"Look deeper Jenni, look with Me again and I'll show you,"* He requested, inviting her to continue. *"Place your hand on the rim once more and you will see."*

Jennifer touched the rim for a second time and understanding entered her heart. With her gaze fixed upon the hole she realised something was missing; something was no longer there that once was. Curiosity led her to reach deeper into the hole, and as she did, she felt something familiar, something tangible with her fingertips that she recognised from her childhood — slime. The kind of slime Jennifer discovered in a party favour she had once purchased at the local fair. She pulled her fingertips back and started to stretch the slime between both of her hands. Jennifer enjoyed feeling the slime ooze in-between her fingers when she squashed it in her fists. She noticed that the slime had words and pictures within its substance. Then unexpectedly the words became audible from within the slime.

Jennifer raised her eyebrows and tried to drop the slime, hoping that that would make it stop; but the slime was stuck to her!

The Fourth Law

"Jenni, the slime represents the self-indulgence you have sort to bring you comfort. This comfort does not bring a cure. You can see that all attempts made to heal the area with your own perceived idea of comfort have only maintained the black holes palliated condition in your heart. None of your attempts have healed the area or bought it back to life. You have only successfully coated the hole and temporarily filled it with a thick goo, a false infilling," He informed her.

"Nothing… nothing is hidden from God. Nothing. You're right, those voices are right... it's time, isn't it? Time for me to deal with this hole. Self-indulgence has stolen, killed and destroyed this part of my heart for long enough," she confessed.

The Cup

"All self-indulgence has done is cost you life; life abundantly." He then showed her a picture of herself seated at the table of the LORD. As she looked at the arrangement laid before her, she noticed that her hand was placed over the golden cup in front of her. When Jesus offered to fill it to a point of overflowing, she responded to Him with two short, sharp words, "I'm ok." She exhaled deeply with great disappointment as she watched Him time and time again offer to fill her cup, yet she refused.

"It's the trade of self-indulgence Jenni; you cannot have it both ways, remember? This is what you agreed to, but don't panic. It's going to be ok. You didn't know, you were manipulated into this agreement. We can fix this. We all want your cup to be filled and overflowing," He reassured her.

The Letter

Jennifer saw herself as an older child, cleaning the outside of the kitchen window for her mum. Quite pleased with the result, she boasted to herself, "crystal clear."

Jennifer was very excited because she had recently given her life to Christ and did not hold back about sharing this new relationship with everyone in her family — uncles, aunts, cousins and grandparents. Today, she was going to share with her mum! She was the first one in her family line for some generations to love Jesus and she desired to give Him her whole heart.

She smiled at her mum through the window. When their eyes met, she pulled a face at her, sticking out her tongue and looking cockeyed. Just as Jennifer was about to skip inside she heard the mail man pull up and saw him filling the mail box with white envelopes. She grabbed the mail for her mum on the way inside and flicked through the pile to see if there was something for her; a usual habit. "Oh goodie — one for me," she bragged as she trotted inside and flopped into a kitchen chair. She held the letter up for her mum to see. "I got one!" Jennifer ripped into the envelope like a race car, tearing around a track. "Oh, it looks like it's from Aunty Jean and Uncle Eric," she said excitedly. They were her two favourite relatives; she loved them.

"Mum, Mum — MUM!" Jennifer squealed hysterically. "What's wrong Jenni? What is it?" her mum replied confused. Jennifer handed her mum the letter and wept profusely at the table. Her mum started to read aloud the hand written words from her aunt on the page. "I'm sorry dear, but we just can't have you come and stay anymore. The Lord has done nothing but bring your uncle and I pain and sorrow. I'm sorry. When you return back to the way you were, we'll be right here."

Her mother sighed in disbelief, "I'm so sorry Jenni." Jennifer rested her head upon her mother's chest and wept inconsolably. Suddenly she pulled herself free from the embrace and ran frantically to her room. She locked the door behind her and launched herself face down onto her bed.

"Why? What did I ever do to them? I tried so hard, I love them so much. How can they cut me off?" Jennifer mumbled to herself. She wailed and wailed until she could wail no more. She was ashamed; thoughts ran through her head that she whispered aloud to the atmosphere in her room. "My own family rejects me. My little cousins, I will never see them again. It's all my fault. I just don't understand. I love them." Her heart could not bear the pain. She quickly became numb and felt like something within her had died. She stared into space, into nothingness.

"Jenni, not like this. Look at Me," Holy Spirit called to her to interrupt the pull from the spirit of destruction. Jennifer was startled by His words and promptly snapped out of the trance. "What now?" she responded in a monotone voice.

"We will go back — together. You will look for Him. He will come. You are wanted Jenni, you are loved," He reminded her as He looked into her eyes. "If You say so," she answered, as the vortex of destruction continued to apply pressure to her heart.

The Updated Map

"Jenni, look at the map of your heart?" She followed the map upward with her eyes as Holy Spirit projected it in front of her. She noticed Jesus' reflection upon the areas of her heart that He had healed. A fire then sparked inside of her and she recalled aloud, "He will heal me... I am loved!"

"Yes Jenni, He will heal you! Yes, you are loved! Don't give into the deception; look at what the LORD has done. Look to what He WILL DO Jenni!" He encouraged her.

The Redemption

"Ask for Him Jenni. It doesn't matter that your face is buried in your pillow," Holy Spirit prompted her.

She breathed in deeply and asked for Him in between her very real tears. "Jesus, I know You are real but where are You? Where ARE You now when I need you most?"

"Jenni, My darling, I'm right here," Jesus responded lovingly placing His hand on her back. In an instant, Jennifer paused her process of distress. "LORD?" she asked. She sat up like a bolt of lightning, still squeezing her eyes shut; then turned awkwardly to the side the sound was coming from, careful to only open her eyes one at a time.

There He was! Blurry-eyed from all the crying, she rubbed her eyes just to make sure she was not imagining it. Jennifer looked at Him again to clarify. "Jesus! You're here!?" She flung her arms around His neck and Jesus smiled replying, *"I am Jenni, I am."*

Jesus tucked her hair, wet from tears, behind her ears and gazed upon His Beloved's sweet face. *"That's better. Now I can see you."*

"So, what happened today Jenni? Why all these tears," Jesus asked while He waited for her young heart to bring forth the pain. "Well... You see..." she began, "I got this letter, and..."

But before Jennifer could finish, tears started to roll down her cheeks once more. She was too ashamed to tell Jesus what had just happened. He put His arm around her and kissed her on the top of the head, *"It's ok Jenni, everything is going to be ok."*

"How? My own family has rejected me, I am simply not good enough! I am so ashamed," she sobbed and hung her head.

"Jenni, their actions are not a reflection upon you, but upon the deep wounds, bruises, callouses and chastisement they have been carrying for generations. They have chosen to not let Me heal them and fill their hearts. Will you let Me? Will you trust Me enough to fix this gaping hole in your heart?" He asked as He stood to His feet and held out His right hand.

Jennifer quickly took hold of His right hand and stood. Jesus led her up the big, white staircase and together they travelled high above the earth. The journey seemed to take an eternity, yet they arrived quickly. It was almost as though the steps on the staircase aligned with moments in her life, starting from the time she was created.

"Where are we LORD?" she asked, looking around in wonder at all she cast her eyes upon. *"I have brought you here Jenni because I wanted to show you where you will help Me rule and reign over time and seasons. Not only in your own life but over the earth and the Heavens."* He then directed her gaze over the vastness of His Kingdom that He allowed her to see.

Jennifer put her finger on her chest and asked, "Me?"

Jesus chuckled and said, *"Yes, you Jenni."* She paused to comprehend what she was being assigned to do and began to ponder what this would look like. The God of all the universe had chosen her to rule and reign with Him.

She looked up at Jesus and responded excitedly, "I will!" Jesus kissed her on the forehead and beamed at His Beloved's progress. He started to explain to Jennifer how things worked in Heaven while they moved about in different areas. *"All things pertain to My sacrifice; the mercy I have established forever from the shedding of My Blood..."* He clarified as they walked along.

Jennifer stopped walking and said to Him with sincerity, "Jesus, thank You. Thank You so much for all You have done for me." She wrapped her arms tightly around His torso. The tips of her fingers recognised the scars on His back through His garment. "Thank You LORD for loving me this much!"

Jesus lifted her chin and looked deeply into her eyes, and handed her a large golden goblet, encrusted with precious stones, *"You're welcome, Jenni, you're welcome."*

They sat and He poured a deep, red wine into her cup which she gladly drank. As He refilled it she allowed the wine to flow out of the cup over her hand, and spill upon her gown, not wanting Him to stop. *"That's My girl,"* He said. *"Drink. I came so I could overflow your cup Jenni."* The wine did not stain her gown, it only caused her to shine, be filled and satisfied.

The Wisdom

I think I've learnt more from You Holy Spirit and the LORD, over the course of the past four steps, than what I have learnt during my entire life!" she boasted.

Holy Spirit grinned at her, *"It's called 'Wisdom,' Jenni, Wisdom. Remember what we talked about at the beginning — when you hate the evil in your heart wisdom can come in."*

"Ohhhh. I'm becoming wiser because I'm allowing You to help me get rid of the evil in my heart — which I didn't even know I had! Wow, when we are deceived, we REALLY are deceived. Holy Spirit I am so very, very grateful," she added.

"On addressing the place of palliation, you were able to receive the fullness of the LORD's blessing and comfort. You recognised that your attempts to 'self-soothe' were futile and did nothing more than place layer upon layer of slime within the gaping hole in your heart. It did not close the hole, fill it or approximate the edges. It simply increased the need for more comfort because what was put into the hole had no means or ability to cure or resolve it. It's fascinating, isn't it?" He remarked.

"It is! I'm just in awe of everything You are teaching me; Your counsel, Your advocacy... Holy Spirit, You are just like what Jesus described in John 14:16, 'And I will pray the Father, and He will give you another Helper, that He may abide with you forever.' You always help me and never leave me — thank You," she exclaimed as she wrapped her arms around Him again.

"You're welcome Jenni. Even though you were unable to touch this part of your heart without Me, you were able to pour paraphernalia into it to find some temporary relief, which in reality would last only momentarily. That was part of your agreement — you would think you were helping your state of emptiness, but really you weren't," He explained.

"Now you are free to receive the fullness and the comfort of the LORD. 'Let, I pray, Your merciful kindness be for my comfort, according to Your word to your servant.[11]*' You have this Beloved. In this fullness, We will fulfil Our promise to you, 'You prepare a table before me in the presence of my enemies; You anoint my head with oil; my cup runs over.*[12]*' Nothing can stop Us from overflowing your cup now"* Holy Spirit proclaimed.

Chapter Five

Step Five: Self-worship

Separation from devotion to God

Jennifer looked forward toward the top of the stair case and wondered aloud, "What do I see?" She peeked back at the previous steps and reminded her heart how far she had come. One, two, three, four steps — and now five! Jennifer began to sway on the fifth step like a child swaying in the breeze. She felt quite at home and relaxed. The top was right there, waiting for her. "I can do this," she declared looking straight into Holy Spirit's eyes. "And I **will** do this."

The Hunger Bubbles

As the words had no sooner left her mouth she felt a bubble rise up in her chest and an intense hunger set in. Jennifer's stomach growled at her like she had not eaten for days. "I ate a good dinner, I don't understand," she said as she pressed her hand against her stomach to try and settle it. A sick feeling formed in her cheeks. "I'm so hungry, I feel sick. What is this Holy Spirit?"

"It is the Spirit of the LORD inside of you hungering to worship Him," He answered. *"Look into your heart Jenni, what do you see?"*

Jennifer saw small bubbles floating all around her — coming from her stomach!

"Examine the bubbles Jenni, touch the bubbles," Holy Spirit instructed her. Jennifer looked at the bubbles as they came from her stomach. They were small like marbles and had a beautiful colour that shone. She admired them. Jennifer reached out to touch a bubble that was right in front of her and it popped. She tried again and again to take hold of the bubbles. They were so lovely, she desired to possess them, but each time she tried to grab one, the bubble burst.

"They just keep popping, one after another. I can't pick them up or keep them, they are futile," she protested out of frustration. "This seems pointless Holy Spirit. What is this about?"

"Jenni, these bubbles represent the worship of self." His words made Jennifer stop and pause. Immediately she ran through her mind all of her Church attendances over the years, the worship songs she had sung while driving or doing chores around the house. *"Look again,"* Holy Spirit advised her.

Jennifer saw focus points, where her emphasis was based entirely on being served, acknowledged and prioritised. She noticed that she cleaved to the places that produced self-worship. She hung her head, realising she had been worshipping self all this time — her agenda, her way, her ideas, her time. Jennifer's heart confirmed what Holy Spirit had just shown her, producing a heaviness within.

*"Jenni, you don't know, until you **know**,"* Holy Spirit reminded her.

The Hating of the Evil

"Do you love this evil, Jenni? Or do you hate this evil? Now that you know it's there, what do you choose to do with this knowledge?" He probed.

"I hate it, I want it gone! I never want to see it again," she exclaimed as tears of godly sorrow rolled down her cheeks.

"See, nothing to be ashamed about — you do not love evil, you were simply unaware of it lurking in your heart My dear." He reassured her with an embrace. Her tears were absorbed into His gown as she pressed her head upon His chest. *"Come now, smile; let's bring this part of your heart back into the LORD,"* Holy Spirit added. *"My dear Jenni, you are a conqueror."*

Jennifer took a deep breath and returned a forced smile. "I don't feel like a conqueror now. I feel like I've let You down."

"Jenni, you could never let Us down, We cannot be let down. We are the God-Head. We are love, We are peace, We are joy. There is nothing down about Us. He holds you up, not down. It is the enemy pulling you down. You were never made down; you were made up. So technically there is nothing 'down' about you — only up," Holy Spirit cheerfully clarified, tucking her lose strands of hair behind her ears.

"You are up, Jesus is up, the Father is up, I am up... just deceived into being pulled down," she reiterated to Holy Spirit.

"Yes, exactly! 'And the LORD will make you the head and not the tail; you shall be above only, and not be beneath, if you heed the commandments of the LORD your God, which I command you today, and are careful to observe them.[13]*' This is all that is required of you Jenni — to listen to Me, to hear Me and attend to what I am sharing with you. If you do not listen or attend to what I am showing you, that part of your heart will remain "stuck" in the place of evil,"* He taught her.

The BBQ at the Pool

"Where did this all start, this cycle of self-worship?" she asked confidently with her hands opened wide before Him. They then entered a gyre which transferred her back in time to a day at her parents' house where she grew up.

She saw herself happily playing in the backyard on her trampoline; flipping, jumping and doing summersaults in the air. She was supervised by her mum who was tending to her petunias. "Very clever Jenni, but be careful, we're all going to a barbeque and pool party tonight," her mum said to jog her memory.

Their yard was not ginormous; only big enough for a few flowers, a bit of lawn and the trampoline Jennifer loved. She especially loved an audience while her mum was gardening. "Mum, watch this!" Jennifer exclaimed as she attempted a double summersault in the air.

Just as her mum looked up, Jennifer landed on the edge of the trampoline and screamed!

"Jenni!" her mum responded immediately to the emergency that had unfolded before her. Jennifer's ankle was throbbing, pain shot up her leg and her ankle felt like it was detached. "Mum, it hurts, it really hurts!"

Jennifer's mum rushed her straight to the doctor. Thankfully, her ankle was not broken, but it was badly sprained. Thus, she had it bandaged for support and had to use crutches for a few days to rest the ligaments.

That night, the family went to the barbeque and pool party as planned. The party was to celebrate the new water park at the local pool. Jennifer was not too upset because she knew she would still have a good time. Until, that is, she got there.

Her parents helped her inside, set up chairs and a picnic rug. Jennifer saw lots of kids from her class, but no one even came to say hello. She looked for her parents, but they were busy discussing swimming pool committee matters with other adults. Jennifer's heart sank... "I guess it's just me then. I'm not important enough — can no one see me? I can see them." Jennifer sighed, then awkwardly navigated her way over to a tree to rest against while she sat on the grass.

The Upload

"I don't understand Holy Spirit, what does this have to do with self-worship?" she asked confused. *"Focus on the emotions of your younger self in this moment,"* He tutored her.

She then engaged with the feelings she was experiencing while leaning against the tree. Jennifer looked deeply into her mind. She could see into her brain and saw an upload taking place into her amygdala, her brain's alarm system for perceived and real threats. She watched as the words 'I am unnoticed and alone; I must attend to myself' were embedded into her amygdala. She now realised that this was the moment she chose self-worship, through controlling the conditions in her life. In Jeniffer's mind, this guaranteed attention, even if it was by her own hand!

"Look again Jenni, there is more to it," He instructed. She re-engaged with

her younger self and looked within the inner workings of her body at that very moment. Holy Spirit took her so deeply into her inner world that she could trace where this information was coming from as it was uploaded into her amygdala. She stretched out her pointer finger to follow the dotted path that formed before her eyes. As her finger made contact with the dots, it was led through something holographic yet tangible. Something that was alive in her soul.

"The words sent to my amygdala came through here," she shared with Holy Spirit. He nodded in agreement.

Her pointer finger continued along the dotted path until she felt a pull upon her finger from a substantial force — her heart. "It started here Holy Spirit, in my heart, I can see it."

"When you sat alone under the tree feeling unattended to and unwanted, your heart did a quick check, to see if what was coming in 'belonged,'" He said continuing to teach her. "A quick check? What does that mean?" she asked needing clarification.

"When that information came into your heart, the 'eyes' of your heart looked around for evidence," He informed her.

"Evidence? What evidence?" she questioned Him, not quite understanding what He meant. He smiled at Jennifer, and responded, *"The eyes of your heart were looking to see if what you were saying was true. Comparing the information coming in with the information stored in your heart already Jenni. It looked and found minimal building blocks of the Kingdom. But it did find many 'ungodly rocks,' so it assumed this piece of information was like those rocks; another one to be added to the pile. This was quite a normal function for your heart — to store rocks."*

"Oh. Wouldn't the eyes of my heart see that I had given my life to Jesus?" she queried Him.

"Yes, they saw that, but, the small 'square inch' foundation, so to speak, that He laid had not been built upon. His foundation of righteousness in your heart laid bare. It had not yet been joined with more truth to build His Kingdom. It was a small silver slab with weeds beginning to grow around it," He told her.

"This is a lot to take in," she responded.

"This is how you grow. This is how you build. You lay a greater foundation, build the Kingdom, His city within your heart by getting His truth in and the rocks out," He encouraged her as He tucked her knotted hair behind her ears.

"'Therefore you shall lay up these words of mine in your heart and in your soul, and bind them as a sign on your hand, and they shall be as frontlets between your eyes.[14] *Do you see here Jenni, the parallel between this truth and the greatest commandment of the LORD? Jesus said to him, you shall love the LORD your God with all your heart, with all your soul, and with all your mind. This is the first and great commandment.*[15]*' Can you see it?"* He asked her, to bring her heart forward.

"I do... I do. He advises us that the best way is to have Him, His Word and His Kingdom in our hearts, to travel through our soul and into our mind, into our amygdala. Our amygdala is behind our eyes and is responsible for managing and expressing emotions and memories that affect the function of our whole body!" she replied with excitement.

"Yes, that's it! Well done, Jenni, well done. And the hand?" He probed to continue to pull her heart up.

"To discern, make the right choice — to listen and act when you hover! Wow, confirmation," she confidently answered.

"Exactly. Do you now understand Jenni, how important your heart is? That is why We have given it the ability to search things out, to see. Ephesians 1:17–18 states, 'that the God of our Lord Jesus Christ, the Father of glory, may give to you the spirit of wisdom and revelation in the knowledge of Him, the eyes of your understanding being enlightened; that you may know what is the hope of His calling, what are the riches of the glory of His inheritance in the saints.' This only comes by building the Kingdom within your heart. Now, it's time to look for Him Jenni. Are you ready?" He invited her.

The Redemption

Jennifer re-engaged and started to feel melancholy. She whispered "Jesus where are you?"

"I'm right here," Jesus answered and subtly asked, *"why are you here, by this tree?"*

She looked at Him with tears in her eyes. "Because I can't swim... since my ankle. I'm left out... even my parents don't care."

"Oh Jenni," Jesus said as He embraced her. *"That's not true, look at Me,"* He declared lifting her chin. *"You are loved by all who meet you. You are lovely My dear."*

"Jenni, would you like to come swimming with Me?" Jesus asked. "I can't... my ankle..." she responded, wondering why He could not see it was wrapped and had not noticed the crutches that were right next to her.

"Not here Jenni. There," He clarified, pointing to the Heavens.

She looked upward in the direction that He was pointing. Jennifer saw a cloud move aside, then immediately she could see the Heavenly Jerusalem. She gasped, as her eyes enlarged from the sight of its magnificence. "REALLY?!!"

"Follow Me Jenni" He stated as He stood up and reached out His right hand for her to grasp.

Jennifer got up immediately without her crutches. Then, when her hand touched His, the pain left her ankle. She skipped alongside Jesus, holding His right hand. Together, they travelled up the white staircase that connected the Heavenly Jerusalem to the earth. When they reached the top of the staircase, Jennifer realised her ankle did not hurt anymore, and that she was not using crutches! "Hey, my ankle… it's fine!"

Instantly Jennifer was aware of the multitude of angels surrounding Jesus and the throne of Father God. Her eyes widened in awe. "Wow!"

She looked silently at them, focusing, as she heard their worship of LORD Jesus and Father God. An unexplainable peace and joy bubbled up inside her, and a river began to flow from her stomach. This river was alive! It was clear, refreshing, and bubbling with power.

Jennifer looked in amazement, running her hands through the water to play with it. She could touch it; it was real! As she engaged with the living water her heart filled with joy. The desire to worship Father God and Christ Jesus grew within her.

She then wrapped her arms around His torso, and as she did, she felt the wound on His side through His garment. "Oh," she said looking up at Him. Jennifer now understood that the water that gushed from His side when He was speared ran through her and beyond as she worshiped Him. She knew that the power within this water gave life and even raised the dead!

In this state of worship, Jennifer felt healed, whole and well. "My heart is for You LORD, for my Father and Your purposes, not for me."

The Wisdom

"You had unknowingly exchanged the rewards and power of this tangible river, on earth and in Heaven, for futile bubbles which had no substance above or below. These bubbles only kept you distracted from the benefits of true worship. Unlike the bubbles, true worship produces tangible fruit such as peace, joy and love, which is filled with power," Holy Spirit outlined.

Jennifer now recognised that the "putting off, casting off" of the evil was a necessity for her heart to serve Him. She had realised that accepting the truth, as confronting as it may be, was essential for her to partake in the Holiness of the LORD.

"You know what Holy Spirit, I'm beginning to become accustom to this new heart thing. I feel the desire and more yearning within me. I've learnt that my heart was created to command my body, His temple, to expand His Kingdom within. I can now be parallel with the Commander of the LORD's army and bring all things into submission to the LORD. For and against no man, willing only to bring all things into obedience to Him," she stated.

"Your heart is becoming the control centre for the LORD. Your soul, mind and body will align in subjection to your heart as you live a life of holiness to Him. No matter what is presented to Him, or His Kingdom, it will not be shaken, rather His Kingdom will shake off all that is not of Him" He said.

"Whatever falls from this shaking will be broken, and my heart will be a place where the tangible substance of the Kingdom lives, like His heart when He was here. I will know I am a 'daughter of God,' made in His image, from

Him, with His Kingdom inside my heart" she reiterated.

"Yes, further shaking removes the parts that don't belong and strengthens those parts that are His through further refining. Now you have something to stand on. The eyes of your heart have something to look at, and know He is what needs to increase in your heart. You now have enough of His truth in your heart to build a landing strip. No good thing will be withheld from you as you continue to do this. 'For the LORD God is a sun and shield; the LORD will give grace and glory; no good thing will He withhold from those who walk uprightly.[16]*"*

"I understand now, the ungodly rock pile in my heart has caused good things to be withheld from me and has kept me from walking uprightly. Not anymore! Now I can receive and build — with You, with Him, and with my Father — as He lights and protects my path." Jennifer clarified with deep conviction.

"Yes, you can Jenni," Holy Spirit agreed, knowing her heart burned with love for Him.

Chapter Six

Step Six: Self-gratification

Obstructing the completion of the scroll

"Jenni, I want to share something with you. Our relationship is deepening and it parallels with something that occurred in the very beginning," Holy Spirit explained as He invited her to sit with Him.

Holy Spirit placed His arm around Jennifer and she snuggled in to rest. This was something she had previously not been able to do — rest. She lived life in a state of wanting to get things "over and done with," to achieve an unknown goal; the "something" that seemed to invisibly exist. It always reminded her that she had to get things done — consequently without love, without peace, without joy, and without authority. But now she could receive the impartation of His wisdom from the position of rest.

"Your heart, and the hearts of all mankind originate in the same state as the world was in the beginning; a place unused, empty and laid to waste. A place of superficial existence that when examined, reveals what is hidden deep inside — destruction, wickedness and ignorance. However, this innate place has the ability to turn, to entrust its complete and full function to Father God, and become what it was created to be. This is Our intention for the hearts of mankind."

"How?" she probed.

"The same way the darkness that covered the face of the deep waters turned in the beginning — I hovered over the face of the waters. I moved and relaxed myself over the darkness, bringing it into a place of shaking from my presence. You know the rest, from Genesis 1:3–4, 'Then God said, let there be light; and there was light. And God saw the light, that it was good; and God divided the light from the darkness.' Father God placed His glory, His throne... His Son, between the darkness and the creation. This is the process of consecration for the human heart Jenni. The human heart was not created to function with the knowledge of 'the tree of good and evil.' That's why the human heart does not recognise that it has stepped out on its own until I arrive."

"Oh, I get it... You hover and You show me the evil systems I am unknowingly relying on that are destroying my heart. Then, we work together to make my heart a beautiful place with Jesus and the Father, creating!" she summarised.

Holy Spirit beamed at her. *"You know, the physical human heart reflects this too Jenni. We also created it to function from the secret place, not the knowledge of good and evil. The physical human heart has cells in it which have the potential to fire on their own, like their own power supply. This gives them the capability to do their own thing. No other cell in the human body has the ability to do this, only the cells in the heart. When the cells choose to fire independently of the primary pacemaker in the heart, the human heart becomes sick. This causes serious heart arrythmias, which can make the heart skip a beat, go too slow or too fast. People can lose their lives because of these arrythmias. However, when the cells of the human heart function under the governance of the primary pacemaker, the heart runs well as it was created to, and the whole person is well. We, the God-Head: Father, Son and Holy Spirit, are the 'primary pacemaker' of the human heart. When I hover and all things come into the subjection of the Word, the human heart functions as it was created to, filled with His Justice, under the protection and provision of the God-Head,"* He explained.

"That's incredible," she responded in awe.

Holy Spirit raised His eyebrows, *"Nothing inside any human being is a mistake or done by chance. All things inside the human being reflect the Father's glory, His governance and creative power. All things were designed to function with and from His Justice."*

Jennifer then jumped to her feet, to take on what lay on the sixth step with Holy Spirit. "I want more light, I want Your hovering to bring light and shake out the darkness within me," she stated.

The Dirty Well and the Jug

Jennifer looked ahead and pictures began to bubble up in her heart. She saw a large jug made of clay. It looked beautiful and had clear water in it.

Holy Spirit told her, *"Pour the water out into the well Jenni."* She then saw an above-ground well in the distance that looked old yet maintained. It had no cracks. It was quite quaint and alluring; a decorative stone water well. Jennifer approached the well with the clay jug in her right hand to pour out the water as Holy Spirit had directed. As she got closer to the well, she noticed there was something that appeared to be moving within it, causing the water inside of it to lap the edges. As she peered into the well, she saw that the water was dark and had large clumps rotating around in it — it looked disgusting!

"You want me to pour this... in **here**??"

"Yes, please do," He answered unswervingly. With her face scrunched up, Jennifer began to pour the clear water into the well filled with dirty, clumpy water. A foul odour arose from the well as she poured. "That's revolting!" she exclaimed. "You want me to keep doing this?"

"*Yes, keep pouring,*" Holy Spirit insisted. As she poured, the clear water ran over the edge of the well and onto the ground. The clear water did not change the condition of the dirty water in the well at all and the odour continued to worsen. Jennifer kept pouring the water into the well; the jug did not seem to empty!

"Holy Spirit, are You sure about this?"

"*Keep going Jenni,*" He asserted.

Jennifer felt as if she had been pouring for hours. Her arms grew tired and she started to sob. "Nothing is changing, the smell is so bad, I absolutely stink right through now. Can I please stop pouring!?" she cried out, wanting to quit immediately to soothe the exhaustion in her body and escape the stench somewhat.

"*You may stop now. What did you see Jenni?*" He probed.

"A well that does not change, no matter how hard I try to pour the clear water in, it still is polluted and stinks — it's exhausting and pointless, Holy Spirit," Jennifer remarked, so He knew there was no point in asking her to do THAT again.

"*You're correct, it is pointless. What do you think needs to happen?*" He asked.

"The well must be cleaned and emptied of the foul waters, for it to be filled with the clear waters," she answered, desperately hoping that she did not have to bucket it all out and scrub the wells interior wall.

"*You are right Jenni, it does need to be emptied, cleaned and refilled. But how?*" Holy Spirit questioned her, placing a demand on her heart.

"Something in my heart needs to change? Can you help me? I really reek and I don't like feeling this soiled." Jennifer knew He would know what to do and that she absolutely could not deal with this filthy water-well scenario on her own anymore.

The Sixth Law

Holy Spirit kissed her on the head. "*Yes Jenni! I can help you. This well represents the self-gratification planted deeply in your heart. Fear, ignorance and an unwillingness to ask are the things that have been floating around in your heart, enabling this 'self' to thrive. It has given you a sense of false satisfaction and has been preventing you from being able to fill your heart with more of Us. Self-gratification has filled this well to the brim. It is full of your commitment to create from your own supply in life, for your own story. You have distrusted the Father's good plan for your life. As you can see, this well of yours is so full of self-gratification that the pure water of the Word is only spilled upon the ground. The desire remains to trust your own story, not the Father's.*"

Jennifer exhaled forcefully, "I had no idea... it's so repulsive and it stinks. I can't believe I did this..." she blurted out. "*Jenni, My dear, remember, your heart does not know that it is damaging itself when it steps out on its own, away from the governance of the 'primary pacemaker,' Us. The cells within the heart believe the lie that because they 'can' fire independently, they should. These cells don't realise they are in fact causing significant harm to the overall wellbeing of the heart and body, when they follow their own reasoning. But now, rejoice! You have responded to My hovering."*

Jennifer respired in relief and started to feel the place of rest arise, accompanied by excitement. *"Jenni, you WILL receive — as you are not looking to the right or left to follow the idol of self-gratification anymore, but to Us. You will be filled, you will receive your promise,"* He assured her.

Grandma's House

The satisfying memory of her favourite soft drink as a child, "sweet passion," filled the air with its rich, pleasing aroma. Jennifer could smell freshly baked goods from a home oven. The combination of these smells soothed her insides. She was at her grandma's house, and was filled instantly with warmth and love. She smiled a smile that went from one ear to the other. She was only 7 years old and she was visiting with her two older cousins for the day. Jennifer loved her older cousins, they were grown up enough to drive and look after her for the day, but not old enough to leave home yet. She thought her cousins were fabulous! A visit to grandma's with them was a delight.

Sometimes, Jennifer would have sleep-overs at her grandma's house. Grandma would tell her about the fourteen angels in the room where she slept. These angels were tangible.

On this visit with her big cousins, they were eating a snack in the kitchen when her other cousin arrived. He was about the same age as the others but lived a little closer to grandma's house than they did. Jennifer jumped up to greet him and hugged his legs and he lovingly tapped her on the head in response, "Hey Jenni." Then something strange happened; something she had never seen before — her cousins began to fight! It started with a heated comment which led to an argument, to what looked like an angry wrestle. Jennifer's eyes widened in fear while thoughts of confusion ran through her mind, 'What's going on? I don't understand.'

Her grandma quickly whisked her away to the room where she would sleep and shut the door. Jennifer could hear more yelling and then a car driving off. She was scared. She looked around the room. It seemed as if the angels had gone and there was something different in the air that she could not quite explain. She sobbed and covered her eyes with her hands.

The Redemption

Holy Spirit then prompted Jennifer, *"Look for Him."*

Through her sobbing she spoke, "Jesus, where are you? Where are my angels?"

"*I'm here Jenni*" He replied. Jennifer then took her little hands from her eyes, glanced at Jesus and burst into tears. Jesus wrapped His arms around her to soothe her. "*There, there Jenni, everything is going to be alright*" He affirmed, tucking her wet hair from tears behind her ears.

"*Come on Jenni, let's go up,*" Jesus said, offering His extended right arm to her and pointing to the white staircase with His left arm. Jennifer always enjoyed every experience she had with Jesus. She knew He could be trusted. She rested her head on His shoulder as He carried her up the white stairs.

Jesus took Jennifer to the throne room and popped her down on the floor of crystal waters, where she saw the throne of Father God and ran to it. "Papa!" she hollered. Father God picked her up lovingly and embraced her, "*Jenni.*" He kissed her on the forehead and asked, "*How are you, Jenni?*" "I'm good," she exclaimed, which was the truth. The event that had driven young Jennifer into turmoil was no longer present. She had left it, she was no longer entrapped by it. She had been removed from the pain and was able to engage with Father God as she always had prior to the event.

Without hesitancy, she jumped straight up onto His lap as He sat down. Jennifer began to swing her legs and started singing a little tune.

"*What do you want to do today, Jenni?*" He asked. She tapped her finger on her chin to think. "Look at stuff!"

"*Then look at stuff we will,*" Father God replied. He knew she loved looking at "stuff." He had created her that way, to be a visual learner.

She and Father God took a visit to the worshipping angels. Jennifer loved to sing and dance with the worshipping angels. Worshipping Father God was her favourite thing to do. These worshipping angels were the ones from the room she slept in at grandma's house, she recognised them all straight away! "There you all are," she said.

Father God then took her into the room where all the BIG books were kept and read by Him. An angel brought her BIG book out and placed it on a tall reading stand. Father God opened her book and Jennifer happily turned the pages. The pages of her book were filled with writing.

"*Jenni, this is all about you, Me and the angels who will help you throughout your life,*" Father God explained.

"That is a lot of writing! How does the writing work?" she asked.

"*You simply follow Jesus and the Holy Spirit and do whatever They tell you, that's all,*" He answered.

The Wisdom

"*'Commit your way to the LORD, trust also in Him, and He shall bring it to pass.*[17]*' This is good progress Jenni, you are growing — this is the most important indicator. When you grow, you know you are alive, not stuck and stagnant,*" He encouraged her.

"For the first time in my life I don't feel like I have to get things over and done with... I feel like I can enjoy them," she added.

The Updated Map

"Holy Spirit, can I see the map of my heart now? I want to see what has changed," she enquired confidently.

"Of course," He answered, presenting the map before her as if unravelling it across a table. *"This is the area you have just conquered,"* He said as He circled His finger around a region along the bottom. As Jennifer looked at the circled area she saw something amazing. It was alight, flickering with the LORD's reflection upon the clear living water that now ran through the region, just the same as the other areas she had conquered.

"Holy Spirit, these regions are now filled with His reflection. But how do I build on them when they look like water, not a foundation as You have taught me? How am I to build upon water?" she questioned. Holy Spirit answered her lovingly, *"Jenni, He is the foundation. 'Therefore whoever hears these sayings of Mine, and does them, I will liken him to a wise man who built his house on the rock: and the rain descended, the floods came, and the winds blew and beat on that house; and it did not fall, for it was founded on the rock.*[18]*"*

She replied with excitement. "He is my foundation! Where He is I can build with Him. The LORD is firm, the LORD is strong!"

"Yes Jenni, absolutely! The eyes of your heart can now see His Kingdom in all of these places. The deceptive pile of rocks is diminishing with every step you take; increasing the landing strip for His love, joy, peace and authority. You no longer desire your heart to be something it was never created to be — the world's. Every step you take removes the rocks, one by one and makes your heart lighter! Every step enables more of it to be protected and provided for properly, guarded by Him. El Shaddai — 'the' protector, 'the' provider. 'Keep your heart with all diligence, for out of it spring the issues of life.[19]*' The evil is present for one thing and one thing alone; to cause you to destroy your own heart. Evil desire will only cause your heart to fail by stealing, killing and destroying all it was created to be, His beautiful garden of Eden. Be hopeful Beloved, your heart is being cultivated into this beautiful place,"* Holy Spirit enlightened her.

Chapter Seven

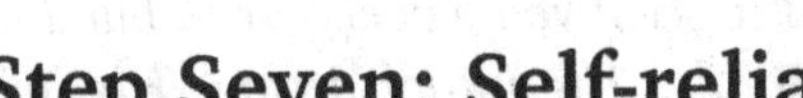

Step Seven: Self-reliance

Turning down your place in Heaven

Jennifer sat on the seventh step with her face in her hands, breathing deeply. Her heart wrestled with the lies inside.

"I've come so far... do I have the strength to keep going? He's shown me the promise, the outcome. I know how this ends, I've seen it..." she reasoned to herself aloud. Her head began to ache and pressure arose from both temporomandibular joints (the hinges of her face that joined her jaw to her skull, which enabled her to speak).

"You know all of this, the promise, the outcome? Do you believe it, trust it to be true?" Holy Spirit quired.

Pain arose between her ribs. Jennifer took a deep breath to try to relieve it, while holding her temples with her fingertips. She then forcefully expired into her hands and breathed deeply in through her nose to maintain a sense of balance. Truth challenged the lies that were held deep within her heart. These lies detested Holy Spirit's presence, and His drawn sword, near the anchor point that secured their vastness in Jennifer's heart.

"I agree you have come so far, but now the endurance given only by Me, the Spirit, will keep you moving forward. The process of removing ungodly trades, contracts, oaths and agreements is not always comfortable. But once it's done, it's done; and the fruit of love, joy and peace always present themselves," He explained.

"It is a necessity to rely on Me to keep going. You must allow Me to continue to discern the thoughts and intentions of your heart. The broad place awaits you; the very essence of your being longs for it Jenni. Your physical body is showing you where you will be freed." Holy Spirit illustrated to her by touching her temporomandibular joints gently.

Renouncing and Repenting

"Before we begin, I want you to understand the weight of what you have been

doing with Me, with Us, during these steps. The words that come from your mouth and your lips when you ask for Him are beautiful, just beautiful. Renouncing and repenting ravishes His heart because this shows you trust Him, and believe that He will do all He has promised you! 'Your lips are like a strand of scarlet, and your mouth is lovely. Your temples behind your veil are like a piece of pomegranate.[20]' Through this process with Us, the sides of your head will be released, and you will become an upright pomegranate tree," He taught her.

"All of this is like a test to see if you will choose to build with Him or continue on with the ungodly rock pile. The initial dream, His invitation to you, will be fulfilled, but only as you are purified through testing. Remember, He is the foundation, that's why you can only achieve the invitation He gave you through Him, by building on Him. Being tested and purified like you are now increases the area for the Kingdom and allows Him to build and manifest — to 'land' His blessings in your heart. Once it's in there, the enemy cannot continue to steal, kill or destroy your heart with the ungodly rock pile," He clarified.

"It's all about the heart, isn't it? My heart is worth so much to Him, to You, to Father God, because that's where His Kingdom is built. It's built in me, in people, His temple. I want the theft and destruction of this part of my heart to stop and the pain in my temporomandibular joints to cease!" she insisted.

"'Until the time that his word came to pass, the word of the LORD tested him.[21]' You are royalty, the Beloved of the KING of kings, you must sit on your throne and function with your full inheritance. You will do this Jenni, with your new heart. I am here to help you pass every test. You will not fail," Holy Spirit proclaimed.

The Papers in the Bottle

Jennifer began to focus on what lay deep within her heart as He placed His hand over her chest. She saw a great expanse of ocean-like waves, with a bottle bobbing up and down in the waters. A cork sealed the bottle's opening to protect the rolled-up papers inside from being ruined. She watched as the bottle was thrown against a dark rock by the waves and smashed. All the papers in the bottle were now soggy and began to sink.

Jennifer then saw herself dive into the water to retrieve the papers. She was not concerned about the razor sharp glass shards or tiny glass splinters that could penetrate her skin from the reckless dive. She retrieved the papers and surfaced with them in her right hand and held them up to the sky, hoping they would dry. Jennifer was unaware of the wounds and splintered areas upon her body that bled from diving into the water with the broken glass.

She then bobbed up and down in the water adrift, surrendering all she had to dry the papers and preserve the agreements they contained. "Why would I desire to bob up and down in the middle of the ocean with no place of refuge?" she asked as her choice looked irrational from her new perspective.

"This is your place of self-reliance in the spirit realm. No place to sit or stand, only an arm to present your statement of truth to the world. The rest of your body is busy keeping you afloat. And even though your body is injured, you do not care for it. You are holding up the abdication of your seat in Heaven and the initiation of your own seat here on earth," He answered bluntly.

Trade Recognition

"Each time reasoning with Christ and trust in Christ is avoided, you have searched for safety and reliance upon self. This has given you a false sense of security and made you vulnerable to attack. The facts are, because of this you are bleeding in waters infested with sharks and other predators without His protection. You are believing the lie that the constitution you have established and hold in your hand will provide all you need in the future," He outlined.

"That is why you questioned me, isn't it? That is why I had the pain in my head. I have traded the secret place and reasoning with Him, to bob up and down in the ocean while being battered, helpless and holding onto what I believe will give me a future. This has left me exposed and bleeding, which attracts predators… I have made myself prey, haven't I? I want my inheritance; I want to sit in the rightful place Christ has purchased for me, I want to live as our Father's child and seek His wisdom. I want His reason with all my heart! I don't want any more of this self-reliance. I no longer desire to be bruised and battered with salt water piercing open wounds and splintered areas that attract predators. I want to stop this trade NOW," Jennifer stated adamantly.

The Ham Sandwiches

Holy Spirit grinned and started to unravel the map of her heart before her. She could see valleys, hills and places on the map where His river of life ran. Holy Spirit drew her attention to the spot on the map where self-reliance held the area of her heart captive. His finger paused over a valley. Suddenly, Jennifer felt as though she was 'zoomed' through time and space to a vast forest of tall oak trees.

She then travelled through the trees to see a group of children playing. They looked to be primary age. She remembered playing on the monkey bars, having pine cones thrown at her face which hit her lip and made it bleed.

Then another picture flashed before her. She was sitting alone on the concrete step eating her ham sandwiches during class time. Jennifer smiled. She loved those ham sandwiches, they were so satisfying! She felt completely content in the moment, without a care in the world. Jennifer was not concerned about being in class, all she was focused on was devouring her sandwiches. She looked around the school yard. It was quiet, there was not another child in sight, only Jennifer and her sandwiches — just the way she liked it. Deep down, she toyed with the idea of attending class but she chose to satisfy herself instead, regardless of breaking school rules. It was easier. In fact, it felt good, right. More to the point, she did not even realise that what she was doing was truly wrong. She had made a choice to eat to be happy on her own schedule, her own time, not at the right time.

"This pattern has kept you from receiving His discipline and is responsible for keeping you from His holiness. It keeps you from your calling and fulfilling His invitation," He stated.

The Redemption

"Jesus, where are You? I can't see You. I just see my sandwich bag and sandwiches." Jennifer had to choose to look beyond what was in her hands to see Him. She then saw that Jesus was sitting right next to her on the cement step. He had been there the whole time.

He carefully wiped a sandwich crumb from the corner of her mouth. *"What are you doing here Jenni? Shouldn't you be in class?"* He questioned her.

"I'll go in a minute, when I'm done," she answered with a matter-of-fact attitude, now attempting to sweep her gaze past His.

"Jenni, you are called and you are chosen. You are required to learn and develop under the watchful eye of your teacher because you are called and chosen. You are delaying learning for the sake of your own idea of security," He revealed.

Jennifer swallowed deeply, now understanding that He was correct. She had made a choice filled only with the potential to cause 'delay.'

"Not like this Jenni, don't keep it to yourself. Use what you have been given or it will be taken from you," Jesus advised her.

Jennifer looked toward Jesus and she noticed something about Him, something different. His eyes seemed to sparkle and He had a glow about Him. Something activated a shaking inside of her; a good shaking, like she was becoming alive. An overwhelming feeling rose up from her stomach. Words started to swirl around in Jennifer's chest like a merry-go-round which she could not stop or hold back. Suddenly, these words forced there way out of her now empty mouth: "Do you have something for me?"

Jennifer wondered what this "calling," "chosen" and "learning" thing was that He talked about. All she ever knew about being called was that she was called names! All she ever knew about being chosen was that others chose her for 'target practice'! All she ever knew about learning was that it was not her favourite thing to do — at all!

His smile widened at her astute question. *"Yes, I do Jenni! Would you like to come and see? It will help you to keep doing the next thing in life."*

She took hold of His hand and suddenly felt like skipping and singing which was quite unusual for her at school. Jesus swung their hands together as they walked up the white staircase. Jesus opened the door to a big, grand library in Heaven. She noticed that this library was different. She WANTED to be there, she wanted to be chosen, she wanted to learn.

Jennifer closed her eyes and breathed in the sweet aroma of the expanse of books on the shelves which she was unable to see the beginning or end of. She ran her little hands along the spines of some of the books. She looked closer around the area and noticed that it was not a library at all; it was a class room inside a library. There were white tables and chairs laid out in the room. But most of them were empty, bar one or two.

Jennifer started to squeeze Jesus' hand tighter and her hand became sweaty. Jesus crouched down beside her and looked gently into her eyes. *"It's ok Jenni, this is the school of The Spirit. It's where those who are called go to learn, to grow, to change and to be trained to pass the tests of life."*

Jennifer began to consider what He had said. She did like it here, but she could not help wondering who else would be attending. She did not want her lip to hurt again like it did when the pine cones were thrown at her. *"Jenni, there is no one here like that, no one at all. All the students here desire to engage with My Justice and learn more about Me, so they can transfer their inheritance and My plans to earth,"* He informed her.

A child approached Jennifer and Jesus. *"Jenni, this is Vanessa. She will show you around and get you settled in. You will love learning here, Jenni, and you will enjoy passing every single test. Here, We value and delight in each and every student becoming who We created them to be. None of you are created the same; you all have different gifts, talents and abilities. I know you will love it,"* He explained to her.

Jennifer began to sway excitedly. She always wanted to know what it felt like to read a big book, to enjoy it and understand what she read. "Would you like to join in now Jenni?" Vanessa asked, offering her hand to Jennifer. Jennifer looked Vanessa up and down; there was something different about her. Jennifer could tell Vanessa had been in this school for a while. Jennifer looked up at Jesus and He reassured her with His smile. Jennifer smiled back at Him, still thinking about the offer.

"Yes!" Jennifer suddenly shouted, before taking hold of Vanessa's hand. Vanessa led Jennifer to her very own table and chair. Everything Jennifer needed was there. Jennifer then turned toward Jesus, and asked, "LORD, where is the teacher?" Jesus came over and sat next to her and whispered, *"I **am** the teacher."*

"Jenni, as your heart opens and is filled with passion and dependence upon Me, you will enjoy learning and find it easy. You will come to understand what it means to be seated in Heaven, where you will rule and reign with Christ — Me." He assured her.

The Wisdom

"You've departed Jenni, from the justice system of self-reliance. You have

turned back to enjoy the journey of your calling, the times of testing and learning. You will fulfil the promise Father God has for you as you begin to rule and reign with Him seated in Heavenly places," Holy Spirit recapped.

"Self-reliance betrayed me so much. It had left me alone, stranded in an unknown water. It led me to believe the lie that I had it all under control. Not anymore. I have His Justice for the pain of the school yard and now I am one step closer to the broad place He has promised me," she stated with confidence.

"Listening and learning under His judicial system gives you the authority and protection you were created to function with. The building of His Kingdom within you is accelerating; it is alive and strong," He told her.

"All I had to do was choose it, believe that He would give me justice for the pain, and act on that belief! I'm so thankful I won't need to take any more pain relief for headaches and jaw aches. The medication never gave me justice for the pain. It just covered over the problem. That's why it kept coming back, wasn't it?" she pondered.

"That's right Jenni. Your relationship with the LORD and His Justice is like a good marriage. Any good marriage always starts with a man proposing to a woman. The woman does not have to say yes. But if she chooses to, she is entitled to share in all of her husband's glory, and becomes one with Him. However, the extent of this sharing depends upon whether she is willing to trust Him — with her whole life or just parts of it. When she gives her time, her affection and her attention to her husband, she comes under His protection and covering. When she tries to pull away from Him and is not willing to trust Him with her heart or parts of her life, He is unable to share all He has with her because she is rejecting Him in those places. In a good marriage, the husband does not leave the wife or the wife the husband; they are one. Self-reliance opposes this perfect plan, it opposes the grace and mercy of God, separating a person from their rightful position to rule and reign with Christ in the land of the living. It prevents them from enjoying His purposes and their inheritance upon the earth," He added.

"Yes... I can feel the power of His glory, swirling and growing within me! I now know I'm in His protection and under His covering. Thank You Holy Spirit for helping me transfer the missing pieces of my heart back to Him," Jennifer exclaimed as she tightly wrapped her arms around His torso.

Step Eight: Self-seclusion

The trivialisation of His Kingdom

"The eighth step. I feel so good," Jennifer declared.

*"That's because the physical body responds with rest when the Kingdom grows within the human heart, as it is brought back into its creative state. The heart remembers who made it, the heart remembers where it is from; and as the Kingdom expands within it, the eyes of the heart instruct the body to enter Kingdom rest. They are finally released to deliver His orders and have the authority to instruct the soul, mind and body to function as it was created to function. What you are experiencing is the outworkings of the scripture in Isaiah 40:31. 'But those who wait upon the LORD shall renew their strength; they shall mount up with wings like eagles, they shall run and not be weary, they shall walk and not faint.' During the steps you have taken so far, you have trusted Me — **US** — and expected Us to do what We have said. You have bound yourself to His Justice system, abolishing what kept you captive. This has changed your heart and relieved it of its heavy load; the 'deals' made with the enemy. And you have allowed your heart to return to the vastness of Heaven — Him. You have removed yourself from areas of toil and exchanged them for the ability to soar like an eagle through trusting and enjoying His Justice,"* Holy Spirit outlined.

"So that's what that really means! It's true, my heart feels so light, I do feel like I'm flying and living from above," she elated.

The Burden of 'Rocks'

"Before, when I always felt loaded up and downcast inside, that was because of the ungodly rock pile in my heart weighing me down wasn't it?" she asserted.

"Correct. The ungodly trades, oaths, agreements and contracts are what weigh down the heart. Not only the spiritual heart but the physical heart too. Everything in the spirit and physical are parallel Jenni. The physical heart also struggles to function as it was created to when these hindrances are present."

"For example, at your age, a person may just feel as if they are unfit taking a flight of stairs; out of breath. However, during the aging process, the 'rock pile' increases, which can cause significant shortness of breath and sometimes pain in the chest. If these rocks are left and never removed with His Justice system, then as a person ages, they may cause the heart to be depleted of oxygen from the increased load. This increased load upon the physical heart, before and after it contracts, makes it difficult for the heart to pump enough blood around the body to meet the physical body's needs. These rocks have the potential to stop the heart from contracting correctly, preventing the heart from relaxing and filling adequately with blood."

"His Justice is all it takes to remove these ungodly rocks and prevent this. A person may look to others to give them justice for the pain they experience in their life, but justice is only obtained through Christ. Everything else is a facade. His Justice is what brings right function and righteousness to all things, especially the human heart," Holy Spirit taught her, adding to the depth of her knowledge.

"That's incredible and so simple at the same time. But… why don't people come? Why don't people search to find this out? I don't get it?" she wondered aloud.

"For the same reason you battled for so long Jenni — the spirit of pride. The same old initial sin: "Did God really say?" Deception piled upon more deception makes the heart hard. Until We have legal grounds to penetrate the human heart amongst all the contracts, trades, oaths and agreements a person has made, and keeps making unknowingly and unwillingly, the enemy tries to make it impossible for a person to see Us. The enemy enjoys robbing the heart of man. He enjoys killing and destroying the human heart. It wasn't until you stated "I give up" that we had any legal grounds to do this. We had given you many dreams, visions and prophetic words, but they all needed somewhere to land. You can't land a plane amongst rock piles and shrubbery successfully, can you?" He answered clearly.

"No, you can't. Pride… I had a lot of that" Jennifer agreed.

The Coin

"Yes Jenni, pride. It is a two-sided coin. One side is insecurity, the other side is arrogance. Either way, it's all pride and it's responsible for all trades, agreements, contracts and oaths that steal, kill and destroy the human heart." He reiterated.

"Jenni, I want you to know, but not only you; I want all mankind to know that He gave His life willingly so you could stand here with Me now and exchange these 'rocks' for His Justice because He loves you. We love you so, so much. He wants — We want — all of mankind to come on this journey with Us. Your willingness to keep standing and moving through these steps shows you are determined to have all We designed you to have, from the sacrifice willingly made for you; for everyone. 'Looking unto Jesus, the author and finisher of our faith, who for the joy that was set before Him endured the cross, despising the shame, and has sat

down at the right hand of the throne of God.[22]*" He always finishes what He starts! He's always watching, waiting for mankind to choose Him. He is faithful Jenni, so faithful,"* Holy Spirit said boldly, tucking Jennifer's ever-changing strands of hair behind her ears.

The Red-Hot Iron

A sudden desire then rose up from within her to run down the stairs and leave; to do anything but go through with this step! "Maybe I should go and do the ironing instead?" she thought. The wicked root deep inside her was kicking and screaming to be left alone and untampered with. The lies started to rush through Jennifer's mind. "This must be avoided at all costs… no one can touch this part of me."

She started to see and sense the presence of a sharp, red-hot poker iron out of a firing kiln. She saw herself place her pointer finger on it, then she quickly removed her finger from the intense heat. Jennifer shook her hand to stop the pain, then placed her finger in her mouth to soothe it.

"Jenni, self-seclusion causes you to point the finger at others… to judge them," He enlightened her. *"Judge not, that you be not judged. For with the judgement you judge, you will be judged, and with the measure you use, it will be measured back to you. And why do you see the speck that is in your brother's eye, but do not consider the plank in your own eye?*[23]*"* She now understood that pointing her finger at others did not remove the source of the pain, it only weighed down her heart.

Jennifer felt the anointing of the LORD come upon her. "Holy Spirit, be my guide, expose this and bring it to the light. It's time I was honest with myself and with You. With all of You," she admitted.

The Movie

Jennifer saw something quite dark. And as she looked deeper into the darkness, she experienced a sharp pain in her chest. All of a sudden, a black, wolf-vampire creature appeared from a movie she watched as a child. This creature gave her the creeps then, and it still did now! Her head started to hurt as she remembered the first time she saw the movie at a friend's house in primary school. She was so scared, she felt as if satan himself had entered into her chest! She was scared to sleep, scared of what lay behind cupboard doors, scared to walk in the dark. She had become fearful and she was too scared to tell anyone until now. "I'm scared Holy Spirit, I'm really scared!"

"Jenni, it's ok, I'm right here, go back to the pain and you will be set free. Divine creation, goodness, truth and humility await you. The fulfilment of prophetic words is on the other side of this step," He said to encourage her as He gently rubbed her back.

The Redemption

"Holy Spirit, where's Jesus?" Jennifer pleaded in an anxious state.

"I'm right here Jenni," Jesus had responded immediately to her indirect call. She jolted and took a deep breath as if He had pushed a reset button inside her heart.

She looked into His eyes and whispered, "LORD."

"Come with Me Jenni," He offered, holding out His right hand.

"I will go with you anywhere LORD Jesus, anywhere," she answered. The LORD stroked her face with His thumb. She smiled and then clasped His hand with hers as it rested on her face.

"My heart, LORD," she said as she brought His hand over her chest to the place of the pain.

The LORD picked Jennifer up and carried her up the white staircase to a room similar to a doctor's office. He shut the door behind them and placed Jennifer upon an examination table. She noticed the atmosphere around them was filled with love and the gentle hum of worshipping angels preparing things in the room for Him. The LORD sat on a white chair with wheels and moved across to Jennifer sitting on the table. *"Where does it hurt Jenni?"*

She pointed to her heart, head, and the middle of her stomach, and whimpered, "In here."

"Ok, not to worry. Let's take a look at that," He replied.

"There it is," He said. He then took some forceps from a tray that an angel was holding and reached into her stomach to retrieve a small, thick, dragon-type creature. This creature had been feeding from the rocks in Jennifer's heart and stealing from her! The creature's aim was to kill and destroy the foundation of brilliant silver in Jennifer's heart that the LORD had laid when she gave her life to Him. Thus, this creature overtly prevented and hindered all building processes of the Kingdom upon the shiny silver foundation of His righteousness. *"I thought so,"* the LORD said as He examined it. He then breathed on it and it vanished.

The Healing

"I am not afraid at all! I have no physical pain either, no pain in my chest, neck, head or stomach — I am free!" she shouted with joy.

Holy Spirit grinned at her, *"Tell Me, what are you going to do with this newness My dear?"*

With boldness she replied, "I am going to pursue His Kingdom and righteousness first, so the 'all' will be added to me."

The Third Sitting

"But seek first the kingdom of God and His righteousness, and all these things shall be added to you. Therefore do not worry about tomorrow, for tomorrow will

worry about its own things. Sufficient for the day is its own trouble.[24]' Come, sit with Me for a while Jenni," Holy Spirit offered. She lovingly rested her head on His shoulder.

"I love You Holy Spirit, I really do and I trust You," she whispered, looking up at Him in delight and awe.

"I know Jenni, I know." Holy Spirit kissed her on the top of her head. "You know, you remind Me of someone Jenni."

"Who?" she asked surprised.

"You remind me of Jacob. Jacob who We re-named Israel," Holy Spirit answered tapping the tip of her nose.

"Jacob? How?" she quired.

"Well, to put it quite simply, your importunate character. Despite all adversity, you are determined to receive all We have provided for you through the victory of the LORD. What people don't always see about Jacob is that he, too, came to this place; the place of working with Me where he persisted in honesty for the condition of his heart to change. Although it was a wrestle, as it was for you, he wanted to enter into newness, via the way We intended — Jacob's ladder. Jacob knew his heart needed the LORD's Justice to receive all We wrote about him. He learnt that he could not succeed with his own self-justice systems. When Jacob desired to connect with Us, what We had intended for him from the beginning of time could be fulfilled. He knew that We had appointed him to the time he lived in, and knew that what he would sow would bear great fruit in the North, South, East and West, as much as the dust on the earth. He too... after many hard life lessons, because of ungodly trades, contracts, oaths and agreements... realised that all of his efforts to achieve what We had promised him were futile. He discovered that his own efforts were not the answer. That's why he too laid them down and joined Me, Us, and entered into Our plan for his life. We did not leave him until We had done what We promised, which was to fulfil his scroll. That's how it is with you Jenni, and Us. We will ensure that every promise made to you is fulfilled. This staircase is the right way, just as it was for Jacob and is for mankind," He clarified.

"Thank You, Holy Spirit. I believe You, I really do," she responded as she kissed the tip of Holy Spirit's shoulder.

"I know you do Jenni. We know what We have put in you," Holy Spirit lovingly stated.

Chapter Nine

Step Nine: Self-dependence

The choking of God's seed

Jennifer quickly drew her foot back from the nineth step. Her eyes were wide with fear from what she had just experienced. "I saw… I saw… I saw myself being choked!"

Terror strained against her to hold its rooted position deep within her heart, causing her physical heart to pound.

Holy Spirit interrupted its process, *"Jenni, look at me."* Her eyes meet His and she started to calm. *"Jenni, you cannot stay here. One foot on, one foot off; it is not possible. You may not retreat, remember, this is a pathway of acceleration. You agreed to this… to give Him your whole heart,"* He reminded her.

"I'm going to die if I stand on the next step! What was there was choking me, trying to kill me?!" she blurted out in a panicked voice.

"No Jenni, no! You will not die. What you saw is what has been happening to you for many decades… the enemy has been choking your heart. This choking will stop as soon as you give Him what lay upon this step. You must trust Jenni. You must trust that He will not let you die." Holy Spirit stated.

Jennifer swallowed deeply. "Will You hold my hand, Holy Spirit?"

Holy Spirit took hold of her hand and she clutched His hand tightly to prepare herself for what was to come.

"Re-place your right foot, Jenni, onto the next step… there is no such thing as 'no-man's land.' It is a fallacy; it is a place of darkness and no truth can exist there. I am right here waiting to help you, but I cannot help you unless you are desiring to stand on His truth."

The Demons and the Rope

Jennifer gently touched her right foot upon the ninth step, followed by her left. Suddenly, Jennifer wailed, "Ahhhh… they're killing me!" She took her hands to her neck as she felt a rope wrench her off the step to hang her. She could hear three wicked spirits chanting, "Pull, pull, pull," as they started to lift her off the landing of the step. They were dark, black shadows; hairy, with vile teeth and destructive eyes.

"Make it stop Holy Spirit, make it stop!" she loudly cried.

"Call upon Him Jenni, call upon Him!" He clearly commanded.

"Jesus, Jesus… Jesus!!!!!!"

Jennifer yelled as forcefully as she could amidst the restriction to her airway. As she called, the demons pulling the rope around her neck seemed to lose their strength, and the task became harder for them as her weight increased. She could feel the tip of her toes brush past the safety of the step landing.

"Jenni, use the power of His name! Use the authority you have in your heart," Holy Spirit coached her.

"I rebuke You in Jesus name, in Jesus name!" Jennifer bellowed with all the strength she could muster. Then, bang! She was instantly released upon the nineth step.

She was disorientated from the experience, panting, weeping and feeling dizzy from the asphyxiation. As she caught her breath, she looked up to glance at Holy Spirit with the rope still loosely hung around her neck.

"Jenni, take the rope off," Holy Spirit prompted her. *"Do you see? They are gone. Finish what you started Beloved. Do not be afraid."*

Jennifer took a deep breath in, exhaled and looked around. "Oh, they're gone. They let go."

Holy Spirit assisted her to lift the rope off her neck. She examined the skin around her neck with her fingertips where the rope had pulled against it with force. It felt abrased and raw. "Is it bad?" she asked Holy Spirit lifting her chin for Him to see.

"It's red… it has left a mark, but don't be afraid. He will heal the area completely and all the pain associated with it." He answered, tucking her tangled, knotted hair behind her ears.

"Holy Spirit, will You please tell me what this is all about? Clearly something evil has been trying to kill me," she whispered rubbing her neck.

The Nineth Law

Holy Spirit gently held Jennifer's face in His hands. *"It's self-dependence Jenni. Self-dependence has one purpose; to choke the spiritual life out of you. As you join with it, it suspends you above the earth by your neck, allowing your lower half to dangle as if you are being hanged. The spiritual asphyxiation makes you oblivious, preventing you from realising that you have handed your authority away through an exchange with the enemy."*

"Look deep into your heart Jenni, right here." He said, pointing to her chest where the apex of her heart rested.

The Butterfly Card

Jennifer was then taken back to a Sunday School class as a 5 year old child, young and tender at heart. She grinned as she remembered receiving a little bible verse card no bigger than a match box, with a Monarch butterfly on it. She loved the bible verse card. Just holding the card in her hand made her heart sing and feel warm inside, but she did not **know** that the Word printed on it had power.

Then, Jennifer was clearly shown a ceramic elephant with its trunk up in her bedroom. It held a sign that stated, "I will always remember." She smiled again as she recalled the cute little elephant, but then started to feel a tightening around her neck.

"*Keep looking Jenni*" Holy Spirit told her. She did not realise that the elephant statue was choking out the Word of God and teaching her that the most important thing to do in life was to remember. She paid homage to the elephant statue daily, quoting it every time she walked past or looked at it. She began to believe that if she acquired knowledge and remembered it, it would set her free. This seemed easy to her; she just had to get smart, obtain the wisdom of the world and remember.

The Second Ignored Dream

Holy Spirit then re-presented a dream to Jennifer of a truck full of thorns that had been pulled from a field. This dream was the LORD's desired outcome for her heart, one that she had not yet sought to fulfil. *"Jenni, these thorns have choked you since you were a child so that you bore no fruit. The seeds We sowed could not germinate because of presence of self-dependence, which continually supported the growth of thorns. You have lived out Mark 4:18–19. 'Now these are the ones sown among thorns; they are the ones who hear the word, and the cares of the world, the deceitfulness of riches, and the desires for other things entering in choke the word, and it becomes unfruitful.'"*

"Self-dependence is a thorn! All these years I have trained myself to be self-dependant, when all I was really doing was choking out what God wanted to do in my heart; what He wanted to plant and grown in my life. It is time for this thorn to go! I want all the thorns pulled out of my heart and disposed of. I desire His riches, the riches only His Word provides. Show me Holy Spirit," she insisted.

The Retrieval of the Butterfly Card

"Jenni, pick up the card again and read," Holy Spirit requested.

She read the words aloud: "For God so loved the world that He gave His only begotten Son, that whoever believes in Him should not perish but have everlasting life.[25]" What Jennifer had gained from this card in her young, delicate heart was that God loved her and that she would go to Heaven one day. Period. It aligned with what she had learnt in Sunday School, that Jesus loved her. No one had ever told her that this truth was just the beginning.

Jennifer looked at the card with greater intensity. Suddenly, the butterfly flew straight off the card and around her room. She was shocked. That had never happened before! She watched it as it flew around her bedroom and then above, past her ceiling. She quickly looked down; the butterfly was still on the card!

"You are seeing the beginning of what His Word will do in your hands. You are seeing the position that is yours, congruently on the earth and in Heaven all at the same time. What is alive up there is alive upon the earth," He explained to her.

"I am alive! His Word is alive!" she cried. She rushed over to her desk and wiped it clean of all the worldly knowledge she had trained herself to rely on, smashing the elephant on the ground in the process. "No more!"

Jennifer was adamant, determined to choose Him. To choose Jesus, the One who is alive, who had made the butterfly come alive! She promptly placed the butterfly card in the centre of her white desk and folded her arms upon it, resting her head on her hands. She stared at the card with delight and intent.

The Redemption

"Jesus are You there?" she called.

Jesus responded instantly. *"You have some questions?"*

Her grin grew wider as her eyes became mesmerised with His face. "Yes. How does this all work? Do You work here on the earth or is it up to me? Am I like the butterfly? Am I on my own here or are You real here, like You are there?"

Jesus held out His right hand and pointed to the white staircase in her room with His eyebrows raised.

"Wow! I never knew there was a staircase in my room to get to Heaven!" she responded in amazement. Jennifer held up her arms to be carried up the staircase.

When they arrived at the top, Jesus put Jennifer on the balcony floor. She ran straight to the edge to take a look. Jennifer grew in awe of all she could see, hear and smell. She looked up at Jesus. "How does all this get to earth? Are there more little cards like the butterfly one?"

Jesus smiled at her wonder, and lovingly patted her on the head. *"That's simple Jenni, everything you need is here. All you have to do is ask. My angels can bring it down the staircase, or you can transfer whatever you need to the earth."*

"Really?" Jennifer was so excited she could not contain herself. "How about a dog as big as a pony?"

Jesus laughed at her trusting request, knowing that she was already planning on how to walk a giant size dog down the staircase to earth. *"I suggest you ask for that one to be brought down by My angels!"*

"Jenni, I'd like you to greet someone," Jesus invited her, directing her towards the throne. She quickly turned on her heels, in the direction Jesus was pointing and she saw a throne of light. "WOW!"

Jennifer began to engage with the light which revealed a figure within it. The figure was a man, but also light. "Is that Father God?"

"Yes Jenni," Jesus replied.

That yes was all it took, and Jennifer ran as fast as she could across the crystal waters to Father God on the throne. She leaned in closely to look at Father God and held out her hand to shake His wondering, 'are You…?'

"Yes Jenni, I AM, the I AM," Father God replied as He crouched down and reciprocated her gesture to shake His hand.

"Pleased to meet you," she said, as she shook His hand as politely as she knew how (because she thought this part of her heart had not met Him before).

"Oh Jenni, we're not strangers. I have always known you, since before you were born upon the earth."

Father God smiled and tapped the tip of her nose. *"Don't you recognise this place? This is where you accepted your mission upon the earth before I sent you there. This is your true home."*

The Wisdom

"Your consecration is increasing the measure of His glory surrounding you Jenni. Isn't it beautiful?"

Jennifer looked deeply into Holy Spirit's eyes and saw her reflection. Her hair had grown inches! It was thick and lovely. Jennifer was beautiful in His eyes and her own.

"Your hair is your prayer shawl given to you by Father God. Which is increasing as His Kingdom expands within your heart," Holy Spirit affirmed. *"Your heart is now living with the dignity, honor and worship it was created to house, and your whole body rejoices, including your hair as it aligns with His Word."*

"Bringing His Justice into the valleys and every other place held captive in your heart allows you to now receive your inheritance upon the earth, Jenni. It is Father God's joy to give it to you. You are now legally entitled to it as you have allowed the Justice of Christ's death, resurrection and ascension into those places," He clarified.

"You are an 'heir.' An heir is legally entitled to a property and possessions upon an ancestor or predecessors' death. Christ died and rose again. Because He died, you, His heir, are entitled to the fullness of His Kingdom in your heart and upon the earth. Since He is alive forever more, He is the administrator of His Kingdom assets. However, as His heir, you will only receive these appointed assets in the areas of your heart that you welcome His death, resurrection and ascension; His victory and His Justice. By doing so, you will continue His work, the work of

the predecessor. The parts of your heart that deny His Justice — His death, His resurrection, His ascension — will they receive the inheritance? No, as they don't truly believe what happened," He taught her.

"So... to truly acknowledge He has died, risen and ascended, my heart needs to believe it or I have no right to His inheritance for me — physical or spiritual," she reiterated to Holy Spirit.

"Yes, that's right. This is written in James 1:6-8, 'But let him ask in faith, with no doubting, for he who doubts is like a wave of the sea driven and tossed by the wind. For let not that man suppose that he will receive anything form the LORD; he is a double-minded man, unstable in all his ways.' Is building on the LORD unstable Jenni?" Holy Spirit questioned her to pull on His Kingdom within her heart.

"No! You taught me that He is the foundation, and wherever His reflection is, I can build with Him! Everywhere His river of life runs in my heart is where I can build with the gold of His Kingdom. I can build upon His righteousness, His silver foundation. He is not unstable; His Kingdom is stable, firm and true. His Kingdom passes all testing of the judgement fire as written in 1 Corinthians 3:11-13: 'For no other foundation can anyone lay than that which is laid, which is Jesus Christ. Now if anyone builds on this foundation with gold, silver, precious stones, wood, hay, straw, each one's work will become clear; for the Day will declare it, because it will be revealed by fire; and the fire will test each one's work, of what sort it is.'"

"What I build with Him, with You, the gold of the Kingdom and the silver, His righteousness... this will not burn or be destroyed in the refiner's fire. Rather, the silver and gold becomes more refined! When His truth is in my heart, my heart is stable, therefore I will be able to receive as that part of my heart is no longer double-minded. As I keep receiving His Justice in my heart, I increase the ability to receive all of my inheritance upon the earth from Father God" she confidently answered.

Holy Spirit grinned at her and nodded in agreement. *"Well done, Jenni; you are accelerating. You will receive Beloved. You will receive all that He died to give you when you keep tending to your heart."*

Jennifer then felt a cool wind blow upon her face and closed her eyes to enjoy the freshness of it.

Chapter Ten

Step Ten: Self-adoration

Veiling the LORD's exaltation

"Holy Spirit, it seems so easy to stand here. Look at how far I have come!"

Holy Spirit raised His eyebrows. *"Yes, you have come along way. You are thoroughly cleansing your heart, which will grant you access to your mountain. You will sit on the throne of your mountain and rule and reign with Us."*

"The truth is, Jenni, you never could've done any of this if you weren't prepared to be honest with yourself and Us. This journey of acceleration brings you into a place of trust, a beautiful and honourable trust. A trust where you are not afraid to be who We created you to be. A trust where you are no longer afraid to exist and live with Us in the land of the living."

He paused for a moment as He presented the map of her heart before them.

"Now, why the cool breeze Jenni? Look at the map and tell Me what you see."

The Mountains, Light and Throne

"It's coming from here, Holy Spirit. This is where my heart has led me. However, there is another mountain, a greater mountain over here with a flickering light that comes on when I look at it. I'm not sure about it. My heart tells me I haven't been there yet — to do the work. The flickering light on the bigger mountain becomes brighter when I look at it," she remarked, shielding her eyes from its projecting light.

He smiled. *"That, my dear, is your throne. Your place of rulership with Us. It has been empty for some time, but now you are on the way to it. Its jurisdiction is vast. It's becoming brighter and brighter as you look at it because His Kingdom inside your heart engages with it and fuels its power."*

The Snowy Peak

"First you must conquer this area here," He stated, circling the snowy peak she had found on the map.

"It shouldn't be too hard. I mean, I'm standing here, right? With no wicked spirits trying to hang me... how hard can it be? I mean so far, I'm not having any manifestations so to speak," she confidently added.

Just as the words left her mouth, snow lightly integrated with the breeze that she had previously found refreshing. She placed her hand over her face to shield it from the snow as it began to intensify. The wind grew stronger, it no longer provided the gentle refreshment it once did. "Where is this coming from??!" she enquired loudly, projecting her voice above the wind.

"From within Jenni. The reason you did not experience it instantly is because of the vast Kingdom area within your heart now. You still will not see the EVIL hidden in your heart until I hover. You must remember, the human heart does not know the difference between good and evil. That is why it stores both, and that is why he sent Me: the Helper, the Comforter, the Counsellor, the Advocate" He answered.

Suddenly, Jennifer became aware of what she was wearing. A yellow snow jacket, navy snow pants, gloves, boots and goggles. She realised that He had equipped her to deal with this. She looked down to wipe the snow from her goggles, and she was instantly transferred to the peak of the mountain she had found on the map.

Holy Spirit showed her that the cause of the storm lay underneath her feet. At once, she plunged to the ground and started to dig frantically in the snow with her gloved hands. She dug and dug; then felt her fingertips brush past an object through her gloves.

The Wooden Box

She immediately removed her gloves and quickly glanced up at Holy Spirit. *"Take it out Jenni, and open the lid,"* He directed her.

Jennifer then pulled at the dark wooden box in the hole. Her hands became fixed in a clawed position; full of pain from the cold. There was a 'pop' as the box released. Jennifer fell backward with the dark wooden box pressed against her yellow snow jacket.

The wind and snow continued to rage against her which now felt like pins against her cheeks. The box seemed to resist every attempt she made to open it. "Help me Holy Spirit, it's stuck!"

The box opened instantly, and in that moment the wind calmed and snow began to cease. *"I am the power Jenni, remember? 'Behold, I send the Promise of My Father upon you; but tarry in the city of Jerusalem until you are endued with power from on high.²⁶' I am the promised One."* He declared.

She forcefully breathed out. "You are Holy Spirit. What is it about this box, though? It looks empty?"

"Thoroughly search the box Jenni," He advised her.

Jennifer found a piece of paper hidden in its lined wall. The paper had been written on and was folded, yet it had crinkles on it from once being screwed up. She unfolded it. The writing on it looked as if it had been done in a hurry. It was very messy — a jumble of signatures and dates. Jennifer wondered why it had been disregarded. It looked important enough.

The Trade Agreement

"This, Jenni, is a trade agreement. This is what created this mountain, this obstruction, and the storm surrounding it," He answered her.

"Did I do this?" she asked

"No Jenni, you did not. You inherited this; but you can dissolve it. Do not be afraid, only be strong and courageous, remember how far you've come. Now, read the document. It's ok," He instructed.

Jennifer searched the paper to find the first words of the trade agreement. As she looked, she started to tremble. Fear began to attack her from behind; fear of what may be contained in the things she read. Holy Spirit was quick to step on the small black demon and destroy it. As her rear guard He pressed her to continue. *"Go on Jenni, don't be afraid... read."*

The cold felt as if it was setting into her bones but she persisted. She read: "Self-adoration." Her eyes continued to scan the page, "I agree to live a life on earth where everything is about me: what I enjoy, what makes me feel good, what elevates me, to become my own idol... I hereby give my estate for the dependence upon this malediction. Holy Spirit I don't even understand this? What does this all mean?"

"It means that you and those before you have chosen to adore themselves instead of the LORD. Because of this, words have been released in your heart; words of evil and cursing, which your heart was not designed to function with. You were all lied to by the enemy. The enemy tricked you into believing that your birth right, Our plans for you, were useless. Just like he did to Esau with the red stew," Holy Spirit elucidated.

"Oh." She hung her head. "I'm easily deceived."

"Not anymore Jenni. Now you have more truth in your heart than you've ever had. This is just another area to tidy up" He said, kissing her on the forehead to comfort her. *"Turn the paper over, look under the terms and conditions."*

She could hardly see them, the writing was so small. Jennifer noticed that the terms and conditions were only signed by one party — the enemy! He had added an edit afterwards to enhance the scope of his trade. She quickly looked up at Holy Spirit in disbelief, "That can't be allowed?!"

"Well, this is how he works. After all, he is the deceiver of all mankind. Please read them aloud Jenni. It will explain a lot to you" He added.

"Ok. Victim mentality... exhaustion... seasons of feeling down cast... hopelessness... robbery of the joy of the LORD... removal of His strength... Oh my goodness! These are the things I have been struggling with my whole life,

Holy Spirit!" Jennifer asserted.

"Yes, they are. This is why this mountain, this trade agreement, must be dissolved. Your mountain of inheritance awaits you. You cannot have access to your assigned mountain without dissolving this. Remember, you can't have it both ways," He clarified.

The Rhyme

"Holy Spirit, what was the trigger?" Jennifer probed.

Holy Spirit placed His hand over her chest, and she felt a bulge protruding from her heart, it was if something had been pulled out and something else had been forced in. She knew instantly that this was the place in her heart where everything was hidden that pertained to the trade agreement she had found in the black wooden box.

Jennifer now saw herself as an eighth grader walking with her friend across the school oval to their "group" in the distance. Jennifer smiled. She loved her friend, she was nice. She had enjoyed spending time with her at Church and Sunday School over the years.

While Jennifer and her friend walked, she clearly heard a group of older boys yell out the rhyme: "Fat and skinny went to war, fat got shot by an apple core." Jennifer's heart sank. In that moment she began to envy her friend. Jennifer no longer loved her the way she did seconds ago. She did not want to stand next to her anymore.

Without delay, Jennifer decided she had to win the approval of that group of boys because she did not want to be a mockery or have things thrown at her like she experienced in primary school! She reasoned that she could not tell anyone how she felt; the shame was unbearable. The words of the boys had mingled with the words administered by 'that man' earlier in the year. The wound in her heart started to draw all her attention and she began to slip into it.

"Jenni, focus, look past the wound" Holy Spirit ushered her. She then saw herself and her friend sitting with their friend group as if nothing had happened. The truth was something major had happened — she had just been driven deeper into the sloughy, stinking wound in her heart.

The Redemption

"Jesus, WHERE ARE YOU?" she yelled in desperation!

He stood right next to her, where she was sitting with the girls on the oval. Jennifer shielded the side of her face from the brightness of His light. And as she did, she noticed His hand was stretched forth toward her.

When her hand met His, tears flooded from her eyes, because the festering wound was now exposed to truth. Jesus embraced her and she pressed her face against His chest. But Jennifer, full of shame, persisted to look down to the ground. He then gently placed His hand under her chin to lift her head, lovingly smiling as He looked into her eyes. Tears continued to flow from Jennifer's eyes as they met His, but the reason for them seemed to change. She started to feel relieved, wanted, accepted and loved in a way she had never felt before.

"Let Me show you something Jenni." Jesus then led her up the white staircase. *"Look,"* He pointed to a room full of babies. The babies were in white cribs, happy and smiling. Jesus walked Jennifer over to a baby boy wrapped in a blue rug and picked him up.

"I want you to hold him Jenni," He told her. She had never held a baby before; she felt a little nervous. Jesus carefully handed the baby boy to her and as he was placed in her arms she began to relax.

She looked at this baby in her arms. He seemed happy, he looked healthy and felt weighty. The babe made her feel warm and comforted. Jennifer began to wonder 'shouldn't I be comforting him? After all, he's the baby.' She bobbed him up and down a bit and started to engage with him.

"Jenni, he's yours," Jesus informed her with pleasure.

"What?! I can't take a baby to school" she replied with surprise, thinking He must be joking or something. Jesus laughed. *"He's your birthright, your inheritance upon the earth."*

She still did not understand and pressed Him for a sensible answer. "I don't get it LORD, I don't think I even know what a birthright or inheritance is."

Jesus smiled and began to explain. *"He is my gift to you upon the earth. He will grow and bring you much fruit and support if you care for him."*

"But how? This makes no sense? He's a baby," she questioned.

Jesus kissed her on the forehead, then raised His eyebrows. *"This one is important and he is going to help you change the world."*

"But how do I care for him? I don't know anything about babies?" she answered, concerned she was unable to do what He was asking of her.

"Look to Me and I will provide everything you need; in time he will grow," Jesus explained.

"Yes LORD, but do I leave him here or take him with me?" she asked, tapping the baby boy on the nose.

"He lives here, but remember so do you. This is where all birthrights and inheritance come from. This is where you will learn what to do to help him grow and manifest through you upon the earth. Your heart is connected to the Kingdom — what you possess in your heart cannot be taken away from you," He advised her.

The Wisdom

"Welcome to life abundantly Jenni. Your previous life of victimhood demanded a response and self-adoration was exactly that. Not anymore though, you are free. Look out to the East and the West Jenni," Holy Spirit encouraged her, pointing

to the area where the snowy mountain had previously held part of her heart captive.

Jennifer followed His finger to where the mountain once stood. It was now a plain of green pasture filled with flourishing life, blooms and light. A warm gentle breeze glided over her face as she released the words, "Ahhh, I love You LORD, I really do," from her heart.

Holy spirit replied, *"'Then you shall call, and the LORD will answer; you shall cry, and He will say, Here I am. If you take away the yoke from your midst, the pointing of the finger, and speaking wickedness.*[27]*' You, My dear, are banishing every prolonged, cruel, unjust treatment you have placed upon yourself and others. I am so proud of you; We all are."*

Chapter Eleven

Step Eleven: Self-manipulation

Discrediting the purity of truth

"Step eleven... I'm certainly NOT going to say 'how hard can this step be?!' I know I am not the judge of the circumstances and situations surrounding me. I know I don't understand evil the way You do. So, I'm going to choose to be peaceful and simply look to You, Holy Spirit, to see what is next." Jennifer stated.

Holy Spirit smiled. *"You have learned well Jenni! It's so important to keep your peace; it is your gauge. Peace is only available in Him and nowhere else. When it seems to disappear, work simply needs to be done with Me to reunite you with it."*

Blood, Sweat, Tears

"They certainly don't sell peace out on the street — it can't be bought with blood, sweat or tears..." she began but paused as understanding landed in her heart. "Oh... I see... I get it! He has paid for my peace! Jesus has **paid** for my peace with His Blood, His sweat, His tears... oh my goodness! I didn't ever get this until now!"

Jennifer looked at Holy Spirit with her eyes opened wide, filled with revelation. "That is why He is the only way to possess peace — He owns the peace of mankind! He OWNS it! Doesn't He? He's paid for it!" she marvelled.

"He does Jenni. That's right! Mankind cannot produce peace; no matter how much blood they shed, no matter how much sweat they produce or how many tears flow from their eyes. He IS peace. The Prince of Peace. It is not owned or ruled over by another. It cannot be bought or paid for. It is simply given in an exchange to relieve one from punishment. It's surprising though how many people would rather subject parts of their heart to the punisher, the enemy, instead of being honest with Us and allowing that part of their heart to be saturated in His peace," Holy Spirit answered.

"I agree. I've seen it and I can now see it in me," said Jennifer

"Once you have made it to the broad place, your mountain, there will still be things to deal with. This is how you increase your dominion on the earth. If you leave parts of your heart out and do not bring them into the secret place, your scroll will not be fulfilled. And He will not have His full reward from your life."

"I want to fulfil my scroll, I want my inheritance upon the earth, I want Him to have His full reward from my life. Everything He paid for with His Blood, His sweat, His tears — I want Jesus to have it all," she declared with unwavering conviction.

Holy Spirit tucked her smooth, silky hair behind her ears. *"Remember, this is a process of acceleration, like an intensive. I know it seems hard at this time, but you will reap the rewards. We promise."*

"The truth is, this is going to be a tough one but please do not be afraid. You will have the necessary victory for your heart. The ground is yours for the taking," He encouraged her.

She silently nodded as her stomach began to turn.

"Excuses have been made, instead of adhering to what is written, to carefully guide you to achieve your idea of an acceptable 'end.' You were made for so much more than this Jenni. The desire to serve the LORD and expand His Kingdom on the earth may only be done through a heart that does not despise His Word. Honesty and transparency with Us are the only way to receive the full benefits of mercy, grace and forgiveness. He is faithful to forgive when you bring this part into subjection to His truth," Holy Spirit revealed.

As tears formed in her eyes, she courageously asked with her bottom lip quivering, "Where did this all begin Holy Spirit?"

The Operating Theatre

They journeyed through a dark tunnel in her heart. A very small light then appeared in the distance. Not just any light; a golden type of light, which was just enough to highlight what was at the end of the tunnel… a very small baby. Jennifer's heart started to pound forcefully and she began to sweat. She took a deep breath to try and settle herself, then asked, "What is this place, Holy Spirit?"

"Keep watching the baby, Jenni," He directed.

Jennifer looked at Holy Spirit with a form of desperation, hoping for the grace to stop. "I'm thirsty," she panted. "REALLY thirsty Holy Spirit, I think I need to take a break," she stated as her tongue stuck to the roof of her mouth, which now felt as dry as sand. She knew she was in a desolate place.

A smell began to rise up into her nostrils. A vial smell. It was the smell of burning flesh from a diathermy in an operating theatre. She immediately cupped both hands around her mouth and nose, and started to gnash her teeth from the turmoil of this place.

Suddenly there was a loud bang! She quickly turned around and saw that the black crucifix had fallen from the operating theatre wall. Panic rose up from within her heart; the whole operating theatre started to shake. The walls began to crack from the presence of Holy Spirit in this place with Jennifer. A rumbling noise then erupted in the atmosphere.

Shame rose up in Jennifer's heart; tears poured from her eyes as if a salty gush of sea water had been released from this veiled place. She felt as though a hot iron was searing the word GUILTY on her right arm.

"Keep looking Jenni," He whispered. A wave of intense coldness then came over her and she began to quiver uncontrollably.

She looked deeper into the scenario and saw herself as a junior staff member, new to the peri-operative environment. A dilation and curette procedure was schedule for the end of the theatre list. She saw the manager speak to her and explain that for this procedure, nursing staff do not have to **do** anything besides set up. She then clearly heard the manager give her the option to step out for the procedure.

It was time for the dilation and curette. The theatre set-up was complete. Stirrups were in place at the end of the bed and instrument trays were ready on the cold stainless-steel trolleys. Jennifer looked at the clock and the eyes of her heart reminded her, 'you still have time to withdraw.' But she ignored the eyes of her heart, and as she did, she noticed that a senior nurse had placed a drape over the suction canisters (containers with graduated measurement that collect fluids during surgical procedures via a tube).

Jennifer asked the senior nurse, "Why?" Jennifer did not understand; she had been taught the importance of accurately recording all blood and fluid loss for procedures. The nurse replied to Jennifer's question abruptly. "It's so no one sees the parts. You know, the parts of the baby." In that moment, Jennifer's heart plummeted, and the eyes of her heart pleaded with her to leave the theatre.

The Brokenness

Jennifer was beside herself — "I CAN'T!" she cried as her feet crumbled beneath her on the eleventh step. She flopped in a heap on the step, broken within.

"My beautiful Jenni," Holy Spirit said as He crouched down next to her, tucking Jennifer's wet, matted hair from tears behind her ears. *"My darling,"* He whispered while lifting her chin with His pointer finger, *"Not like this. Remember who you are — 'Ours.'"*

Jennifer took a deep breath in and wiped her face with her hands. "I think I'm going to throw up Holy Spirit, I don't feel well," she mumbled.

"Let Me help you. I won't fail you and neither will He," Holy Spirit reminded her. He wrapped His arms around her torso, gently lifting her to her feet to conquer what lay on the step. *"That's better, My darling,"* He said, stroking her

cold head with His hand.

The warmth of His hand bought welcomed relief. *"Jenni, I want you to go back and see the battle the eyes of your heart are having."*

The Spirit of Death

Jennifer went back into the scenario. She could see her spiritual heart. She then saw that the eyes of her heart had taken inventory of her heart's contents. They had found ungodly rocks within it that had the ability to connect with murder — rocks of hatred.

Then she watched as the eyes of her heart became silent, in response to what they had found.

Holy Spirit then revealed to Jennifer the presence of the black spirit of death, roaming freely in the operating theatre. It had no features, only darkness. She saw it whisper into her right ear, "You can stay. This is about science. This is about preserving the quality of life for the mother. This is not about the contents of the womb." Her weeping increased as she saw her head nod ever so slightly to comply with 'its' words.

The woman was then wheeled in. Jennifer was unable to look away, frozen yet drawn to what was unfolding before her. Jennifer's eyes widened in shock as she learned that the woman would remain conscious for the procedure.

Jennifer's ears heard the conversation in the operating theatre, and watched the interactions within the room amongst the patient, staff and the spirit of death. The staff voiced everything 'it' whispered into their ears, transferring its words immediately to the woman as they tapped her right hand in a loving fashion. "You're doing the right thing."

A numbness came over Jennifer as the woman's legs were placed in the stirrups. Then Jennifer heard more words from the spirit of death and reinforced them by whispering the words she heard aloud: "I'm only observing."

In that moment, Jennifer learnt that she, the staff, and the baby's mother had elected this innocent, unborn babe to pay the price of 'justice' for her mother's pain. They had all partaken in this grievous sin, the shedding of innocent blood.

The woman was then wheeled off to recovery and the usual theatre cleaning process began — just as if murder did not take place in the room. Just as if no one had been repeating the words from the spirit of death, giving 'its' words permission to exist and function.

Jennifer quickly left the theatre to go to the rest room to wash her hands. They were covered in blood — invisible blood — which dripped on the floor, following her. "I am a murderer!" the eyes of her heart screamed at her with the dirtiness of the bloodshed she had participated in! She looked in the mirror on the wall, all she could see was guilt; in her eyes and on her hands. She bashed her head against the glass, as the rocks of hatred and murder grew in her heart. "Why did I stay????"

The Eleventh Law

"*Self-manipulation,*" Holy Spirit stated bluntly. "*It was able to get a hold on you from the rocks within your heart. The moment you gave your ear to the spirit of death — you believed 'its' word above Ours,*" He explained.

"I am such a hypocrite! I gave my ear to the enemy and agreed with him so he could empower his kingdom through the shedding of innocent blood!" she howled, appalled by what she had seen within herself.

"I want this gone and I want it gone now Holy Spirit! He didn't create me for this. I will never fulfil His gracious invitation with this inside me. I want Christ to be LORD of my whole heart, to bring delight to Him," she urged.

"*This is exactly why I was sent. 'And when He has come, He will convict the world of sin, and of righteousness, and of judgement.*[28]' *You are working with Me to admonish the agreements you made with the spirit of death that day — from the listening of your ear, the nod of your head, and the words that left your mouth. Now, look for Him Jenni,*" Holy Spirit instructed.

The Redemption

"Where are You LORD?" Jennifer's eyes began to search for Him in the operating theatre. She then saw Him next to the woman on the table. His left hand was on the woman's lower abdomen, over her womb, while His right hand rested upon her knee in the stirrup. Jennifer watched Him and began to listen closely. Then Jesus spoke to the unborn baby girl in her mother's womb.

Jesus declared His love for her, and reminded her that it was His joy to shed His Blood, His sweat, and His tears for her, as well as for her mother. Jennifer saw the unborn baby girl smile in her mother's womb. The baby girl knew how much He loved her, even though there was an insult about to take place upon her very presence in her mother's womb. The baby knew she was a warrior, made by Him, sent by Him. And she reiterated to Him that she was prepared to fight this battle until the end. After all, she knew the inside of her mother's womb better than the surgeon.

Jesus told her how sorry He was for the battle that was about to be forced upon her that she would not win. He let her know that He was ready and willing to give her mother justice for all her pain, as soon as she asked, including the pain she would have from what she was about to do.

The unborn baby girl smiled at Jesus as He reminded her of the book she agreed to complete before Father Gods throne, when they reasoned together about her mission upon the earth. The unborn baby knew she was made to grow, to live, to love and to teach. He reassured her that He would not leave her side as she walked through this valley, this shadow of death, and guaranteed her that Father God would receive her straight back into His Kingdom. Lastly,

Jennifer heard Jesus make a promise the unborn baby girl — His will for her life upon the earth, would be done.

"How?!!" Jennifer yelled out across the operating theatre to Jesus, looking straight at Him with tears streaming down her face. "This baby girl is about to be murdered!"

Jesus gently smiled and replied, *"I will give her justice for the pain of what is done today. I have paid in full for her justice."*

Jennifer was given divine understanding from the LORD. His will for her life, for everyone's life, was for all to receive and live from His Justice. She now knew that life on earth was not an endless safari of searching for His will, but rather to receive and engage with His Justice. She now knew that this IS His will... for **all** to engage with His Justice... this fulfilled peoples scrolls, their books written in Heaven.

Jennifer quickly became overwhelmed in this moment of His great, GREAT Holiness, His thoroughness and care for everyone He created, including the unborn. She immediately took this pearl of absolute wisdom and stored it in her heart. She knew she would never forget that it was His will for her and all of mankind to receive His Justice in their lives, in their hearts.

Jennifer was humbled to her core, knowing that God Almighty loves her THIS much. She began to flop and fall from the heaviness of this revelation in her heart! Before her knees completely gave way, she felt Him lift her chin toward His face. She grievously looked back at Jesus with guilt heavily weighing upon her, now understanding that she had sinned against this perfect man, this perfect God, Christ Jesus and His perfect creation.

His eyes began to pierce Jennifer's with His burning love, a passion that seemed to sear away all the guilt, the shame, the chastisement, the bruising, the wound and the callous. She felt light, completely surrounded by His tangible, peace, love and joy.

'Why?' she wondered. Jesus, knowing her thoughts, said, *"My Justice is for all who acknowledge their sin. My Justice came to give life, not to destroy it. I have paid for you to have My Justice in this piece of your heart Jenni. I have **justice** for you."*

Without delay, Jesus extended His hand to Jennifer. Jennifer took His hand straight away and instantly received His Justice. Jesus smiled at her as He said, *"Come on Jenni, this is going to be powerful."*

She then followed Him up the white staircase. With each step she took, she felt her breasts fill, just as they had when she fed her own children upon the earth. A word from heaven gently landed upon her heart: "nurture."

They arrived outside a large, white door which He pushed open proudly. There was a room full of babies, as far as her eye could see! The babies were happy, healthy, at different ages and stages. Tears of joy gently ran down Jennifer's cheeks from the beauty of it all. Angels tended to the needs of the babies, with the assistance of each of their relatives that had gone before them. Jennifer was instantly in awe of the deep love and intimate knowledge the LORD had for each and every one of them.

"There are so many of them LORD," she said as she rested her head upon His shoulder.

"I know Jenni. I have given each of them My Justice. They are Mine. Their plans will not go unfinished upon the earth. I will ensure they are fulfilled through the generations to come after them, within each family line. In the last days, I will raise them up to rule and reign with Me."

The Wisdom

"Holy Spirit, is this why I would vomit all day once a year for no apparent reason?" she asked.

"Yes, you were never the same after that. Now, all things are made new! That part of you is back in the secret place where it belongs," He joyfully announced.

♥

Chapter Twelve

Step Twelve: Self-dedication

Forsaking the LORD to satisfy self

"Jenni, what do you see now?" He queried her.

"I see a vast city on a hill, surrounded by a golden light that penetrates and illuminates the buildings, the trees and the roads that surround it. It's so bright it nearly looks like it is on fire, like a fiery sunrise," she described. A gentle refreshing breeze flicked at her hair which caused it to glisten, as if to magnify the glory of the LORD she was now carrying.

Holy Spirit kissed her on the top of her head. *"Jenni, you are looking at the city the LORD has put you in charge of. Remember, a city on a hill cannot be hidden."*

"This is mine," she whispered with confidence.

"It is. It is assigned to you and you alone. Would you like to take ownership of it Jenni?" He asked.

"I thought you said it was mine?" she questioned Him, somewhat confused.

"It is, but in any case, to purchase a property an exchange has to happen between the buyer and the seller. This has been purchased for you through the Blood. But until now you have not been in the right 'financial' position to acquire it" He explained.

Perplexed, Jennifer replied, "What do you mean? I thought we came without money and received. You know, as it's written in Isaiah 55:1: 'Ho! Everyone who thirsts, come to the waters; and you who have no money, come, buy and eat. Yes, come, buy wine and milk without money and without price.'"

"Yes, this is true. However, the exchanges one makes throughout one's life with the opposition and the LORD are in fact 'financial' agreements. The godly finance of your life is faith and trust in His Justice and promises. Until now, your 'purse' has been rather empty of this finance. Everything is free in the Kingdom from the trade of the things of the world such as money and deception. Nothing can be purchased from the Kingdom of Heaven and transferred to the earth without faith and trust in His Justice system and promises" Holy Spirit reminded her.

"Oh. I now possess Kingdom wealth which will not be taken away from me because I have been building on Him right, on His truth?" she clarified.

"You are correct. Is not that the reason why Jesus said He came? 'The thief does not come except to steal, and to kill, and to destroy. I have come that they may have life, and that they may have it more abundantly.[29]*' Your purse was empty because your heart had been stolen from profusely by the opposition in order to kill and destroy it, by means of every deceitful agreement you knowingly or unknowingly made with him. Including those hinderances you inherited. But NOW, your purse is filled with the currency of His Kingdom. NOW you engage in abundance; the abundant life the Blood purchased for you,"* He explained.

"Oh! I need to keep filling my purse, my heart, with His Justice, His Peace and His promises, to keep purchasing the abundance of Heaven and bringing it to earth. When I empty my heart of the deceitfulness of the world and its ruler, in exchange for His Justice, I receive abundant Kingdom wealth," she recapped.

"That's right! So now that you know you have Kingdom currency in your heart, what are you going to do with it?" He questioned her.

"I'm going to use its equity to purchase what has been promised to me! I'm going to start by asking you what I have pledged, traded or agreed to that has deceived me into the loss of my city... and yes, I know what You tell me may make me feel uneasy but I want my full inheritance upon the earth. I want my LORD to have His full reward from my life," she announced.

The Map Overview

He rolled out the map before her. *"You've taken this ground here. You can see that the snowy mountain is gone, this region here has been cleared, and now we will take back your city, which is right here. It's not far from your mountain,"* He told her, circling His finger here and there over the corresponding areas.

Jennifer reviewed the positions on the map, sweeping her eyes across its entirety. She recognised the areas of her heart that had received His Justice because they looked the exact opposite of the ones that remained. "It's close... as I look Holy Spirit, I feel His love so heavily, so much peace, so much abundance... yet there is more ground to take?" she queried.

Holy Spirit paused to acknowledge her heart. *"Yes Jenni, there is more. Don't forget, this consecration process is doing more than you can see or feel in the present moment. There are parallels occurring upon the earth and in Heaven because of this process. This will not only change your life, it will change the lives of others as you sweep the area clean of all contaminants. Just as Cyrus set the Jewish people free from decades of captivity, bringing them back to their promised land, you will do the same. Once you have conquered the region on this map, there will be another to conquer. This is how you rule and reign. The opposition will rise and he will fall. As long as you keep the regions given to you in the rulership and abundance of the Kingdom, I will always help you to maintain this position. This is why I was sent, to help you keep your land under the governance of Heaven, to teach you how to rule and reign. It is, as you know, the spiritual war written in Ephesians 6:12: 'For we do not wrestle against flesh and blood, but against principalities, against powers, against the rulers of the darkness of this age, against spiritual hosts of wickedness in the heavenly places.'"*

The Black Cloud

Jennifer saw a thick, black cloud; thicker than any smog upon the earth blanketing the light of her city. The cloud made her feel sick in her stomach.

"What is that?" she asked Holy Spirit.

"That, Jenni, is the result of an ungodly trade — self-dedication" He answered.

"Self-dedication? I thought I had been dedicated to God?" she asked, because she could not see in the dark.

He gently placed His hand over her heart. *"Look again... what do you see?"*

Jennifer's Engraved Heart

She then felt the cloud of darkness pierce her heart. "Ouch! I see the cloud inscribing on my heart..." Jennifer said, clutching His hand that was over her chest. "I can see a script now... I can read what it says. I can see a demon in the cloud, engraving this script upon my heart. Owo... my heart bleeds as it engraves, like a tattooist, yet deeper. I am laying there willingly letting it do this to me. Why, Holy Spirit? Help me!" she called, beginning to wail, knowing that a dark, cloudy demon had been carving on the walls of her heart.

"What does it say Jenni?" Holy Spirit probed, encouraging her to continue on.

With tears she begrudgingly looked again and read the words engraved on the wall of her heart aloud. "I have given it permission to improve my appearance, to be an ornament, an embellishment for me... it has been sworn in as the incumbent in this area of my heart. Holy Spirit, help me. I don't know what to do!"

He reassured her with a smile, *"You do know what to do. Ask me where this trade came from."*

The Song

Straight away, she could see herself at a friend's house after school. There was a group of them from her class. She then saw her friend's older brother come out of the house and jump into his car to head out. Jennifer and her friends watched him as he revved up his car to show off in front of all the girls. They rolled their eyes at him and continued on with their conversation above the engine noise. Out of the blue, he took his foot off of the accelerator, opened his car door and blurted out to Jennifer in front of everyone, "Hey Jenni, this is for you." He played a song with the lyrics 'Big Rear Girls' and started violently laughing at her. He then shut his car door and drove off like a hoon down the road.

Jennifer was stunned, humiliated and embarrassed. Not a word was spoken in response by her friends. It was as if they had a pledged moment of silence to pay homage to his words.

Her heart began to race. 'What am I to do now?' she thought. She had been exercising profusely and had begun skipping meals to lose weight so that she would fit in. The only way Jennifer knew how to recover was to force herself further and further into the mould of the world.

Jennifer could see that she did not react on the surface to his words, but the eyes of her heart responded immediately. The eyes of her heart looked within and saw the rocks that reinforced her friend's, older brother's hurtful words. The words from 'that man,' the words from the older boys at school, and now these words — another rock to add to the pile that already stole so much from her.

She now knew that this was the very moment that the cloudy demon engraved those words upon her heart with its hot, searing blade. The pain within her heart was unbearable, but she had agreed to the wound, the searing, because she wanted to be accepted by men. Jennifer did not want to be alone, hated, mocked or abandoned. Jennifer wanted to be loved.

The Redemption

"Jesus, where are You? ARE you here?" She looked around her friend's yard, near the car and driveway, and near her friends. He was not there. "Where then? Why are You not with me?" she questioned Him aloud, in His foreseen absence.

Then, instantly, time, sound, and noise stopped. Everything stopped! Everything, except Him.

"Jenni, I'm here" He said. His voiced started to penetrate the hardness of her heart from the engraving.

The affected area of her heart was tender to touch. It was swollen; its walls were infected and hard like concrete. She exhaled to try and breath out some of the 'infection.' Jennifer then started to consider what it would be like to allow Him to have THIS part of her heart, for it to receive His Justice, His Peace — His rest.

She glanced around the scenario. There was nothing alive in the scene except them — her and the LORD. She looked again and it started to fade away into nothingness; fragments of the scene simply fractured and dissolved, as if it was never there. She looked back at Jesus and noticed He was smiling at her.

"What do you think now Jenni?"

"You are LORD of ALL... LORD of every living thing; EVERY breath, every time, every season and every event." Jennifer answered Him confidently.

"I am indeed Jenni, and I am the LORD of this pain in your heart." He added with authority. As He spoke, His words penetrated her heart where the searing hot blade of the demon had engraved on its wall.

Holding out His right hand, He said: *"My arm is not too short to save, nor My ear too far to hear."*

She felt the area that had been engraved start to heal from the inside out, until the tissue returned to its original form, full of light and life. No scar remained. Her heart was no longer heavy or hard like concrete.

The Art Room and Stella

She clasped His hand and journeyed with Him up the staircase, leaving behind the betrayal to her created self from the trade. The LORD took her into a room that looked like the art room at her school, but even more 'arty.'

Father God was present. *"Hello Jenni"* Father God said as He lovingly smiled at her from across the art room. He was looking at some plans with angels.

"Hello Papa" she replied.

Father God walked toward Jennifer and rested His arm around her shoulders and said, *"I'm so pleased you could be here today Jenni. What you're about to witness is incredibly important to all of Us."*

The room had more tools than Jennifer had ever known, it was filled with glorious music and a wonderous light. It felt like a place of birth and a place of absolute beauty. She saw two bright spot lights on golden stands, which were crafted with golden leaves and flowers and embellished with jewels. These lamps were focussed on a man-sized lump of clay. She received a knowing that this clay had infinite worth to Father God. It was surrounded by angels with blueprints and the tools required to complete the design. "LORD, who is the artist? The craftsman of this marvellous piece?"

Father God grinned at her and raised His eyebrows. She noticed Father God's expression enter into a state of indescribable wonder. She then received a knowing and understanding of how much They love creating. How much They love building the temples the Spirit will abide in — 'His people.' Their love for this one radiated out from deep within, with an intensity that filled the art studio and all of Heaven.

An angel presented the LORD with the blueprints Father God had completed, and another angel presented a tray of tools for the design. He smiled at the angels and thanked them. Jennifer watched carefully as she saw a human form created in the clay from His craftsmanship. Another angel came with a tray that glowed with light. The LORD carefully picked up the light source that rested on the tray and placed it on the left side of the chest of the clay human form. He smiled and turned to Jennifer with His hands on His knees.

"Jenni, this is 'Stella.' She is one of Our most wonderful creations. Her heart

will change the hearts of men. I will put My Spirit in her. Every part of her is designed and fashioned by Us to complete the assignment We have given her."

Jennifer saw the incredible woman 'Stella' would be and all Father God had planned for her. Jennifer was only able to respond with "Wow!" Jennifer relaxed and felt a weight come off of her shoulders and asked "Did…" but before she could finish, Jesus responded, as He knew her thoughts. *"Yes, We did… and yes, We have,"* He said smiling at her.

Jennifer watched as Jesus drew her attention to the light He had placed within Stella's chest. Father God breathed on the light and Stella's whole-body illuminated, and excess clay fell from around her human form. It was as if the clay and the blueprints that were created just for her worked supernaturally together to fulfil His image. Their perfect unique creation.

Jennifer looked intently at Stella, acknowledging Father God's incredible, perfect work and flawless finish. Every part of Stella was made in His image. Jesus walked up to Stella and kissed her on the forehead. *"My Beloved."*

Stella then opened her eyes. "My LORD," she answered.

Tears of delight softly ran down Jennifer's cheeks from what she was witnessing.

"Jenni, come and meet Stella," He prompted.

"Hello Jenni, it's nice to meet one of my sisters." Stella said, greeting Jennifer with a welcoming smile.

Jennifer exhaled deeply into her hands, astounded by the beauty of her sister. Jennifer quickly took her hands away from her mouth and said, "Hi Stella, you have an amazing smile."

"I see you have been made like me," Stella noted, pointing to Jennifer's human form. Jennifer looked herself up and down at once, not quite understanding what Stella was referring to.

"You know, perfectly original, in His image," Stella explained. Jennifer looked again at her own arms, her legs and touched her stomach, her face, her hair and suddenly realised… Stella, her beautiful sister, was right!

"Yes Stella! I too am made in His image, just like you," Jennifer replied.

Jennifer hugged Stella, knowing that she was just like her, made perfectly in His image. "Thank You LORD… thank You for showing me all of this. I have to ask, can…" but before Jennifer could even finish her question, the LORD breathed on her, infusing her with an even greater light for her assignment upon the earth. Jennifer's body glowed with His light.

The Wisdom

Jennifer opened her eyes and looked around. She was standing in the midst of the city that she was unable to possess earlier! It was now hers!!

"Well done, Jenni, it is yours," Holy Spirit said, embracing her. *"'Let your light so shine before men, that they may see your good works and glorify your*

Father in heaven.[30]"

"Holy Spirit, I want to know, how does it happen? How does He pause everything and make scenarios dissolve in that way?" She questioned Him, looking for an imminent answer.

"Simply Jenni, He can do it because He is LORD over everything and He IS Justice, remember?" Holy Spirit reminded her again.

"I know, but HOW? I want to know more... please Holy Spirit?" she persisted.

Holy Spirit then presented two parallel lines before her eyes and named them. *"This is line 'a,' His Kingdom,"* He said, pointing to the line above, *"and this is line 'b,' the kingdom of the enemy,"* pointing to the line below. *"When a person makes an agreement with the enemy, part of their heart is removed from line 'a,' and transferred down to line 'b.' That part of their heart will stay on the trajectory of line 'b,' bound to the path of the opposition until the person asks for His Justice; justice for the pain that drove them into the ungodly agreement. The time that elapses along line 'b,' may be as short as minutes to days, or as long as decades to half a century or so. When a person 'stuck' on line 'b' asks for His Justice for the pain, that person is retrieved from the exact point in time along line 'b' where the ungodly agreement was made. He instantly dissolves everything that was attached and associated with the ungodly agreement from that very point in time as if it had never existed. You know 'Ab initio' — it 'never' existed on earth or in Heaven! Then the person is automatically transferred by Him straight up to line 'a,' and continues on to fulfil His purpose for them as if they had never been on line 'b.' He is the ONLY ONE in the entirety of the universe that has the power and ability to do this. That is why He is KING of kings and LORD of lords. He **is** above all"* Holy Spirit taught her.

"Wow, that's incredible! I believe it to be true; I know it's true! I am experiencing it to be true with every step I take," she declared to Holy Spirit. "Thank You LORD Jesus, my KING!" she shouted, thrusting both her arms in the air to give praise to Him!

Step Thirteen: Self-conservation

Place holding the glory of the Cross

Holy Spirit held out His hand to assist Jennifer onto the thirteenth step. She clasped His right hand and stepped up, like a bride to the altar on her wedding day.

"How do you feel?" Holy Spirit asked.

She paused for a moment, reflecting on all she had been through with Him. "I feel like I have entered rest. Like I have a new beginning full of potential. I'm understanding the reality of His Kingdom in me and its connection to His throne. It's almost intoxicating!"

He chuckled. *"That potential that you're feeling is real. It's the power of Me, of Him, swirling inside your inner most being, within your heart, bringing everything you were sent here for to pass in this very moment."*

"Everything?" she questioned.

"Yes Jenni, everything," He said, tucking her hair as He always did, behind her ears. *"You see from the moment you gave your life to Christ, you had access to everything. You just had to take back the land that the opposition had withheld from you. Now Jenni, as you approach your mountain, your position of rulership upon the earth, all things are there for the taking. The obstacles are diminishing,"* He outlined.

"The evil and the calamities that you passively kept in your heart which caused it to be diseased have lost their power. No more mischief or neutering of Our seed in your heart! Your heart has become convinced that His Blood has given you justice. The eyes of your heart look around from left to right and confirm that this is true; they see His truth and His Kingdom, holding a strong position in your heart and continuing to multiply. Just as it is written in Hebrews 10:22: 'let us draw near with a true heart in full assurance of faith, having our hearts sprinkled from an evil conscience and our bodies washed with pure water.'" He said, gently holding her delicate face of light in His hands.

"The Kingdom of God IS IN you Jenni. This is what Jesus spoke of in Luke

17[31]: 'The kingdom of God does not come with observation; nor will they say, see, here!' or 'See there!' For indeed, the kingdom of God is in within you.' He is the Kingdom of God and He has, and continues to, expand His reign inside your heart. Your heart has entered His rest and from now on, this rest will only increase as you scrupulously remove the insidious things that remain. Their reign has come to an end, but we must keep cleaning so these things will be permanently removed from your heart."

"So, this is what You really feel like inside me. The Kingdom: energised, excited, full of hope, love, and ready to engage with the potential of Heaven" she commented, marvelling at all He had said.

"Yes, this is life abundantly," He replied.

The Mop Up

He brought up the map of her heart. *"This is our current course of action. We are here."* He then encompassed all the areas on the map they had taken from step one to step twelve with His hand.

"All of this, that was once occupied by the enemy, has now lost its power; but we must not leave any stone unturned. This is not just for you but your future generations too. If these things are left to lay waste on the ground, they will maintain the potential to, let's say, 'sprout and grow,' if triggered by events in the future. As you can see there are clearly four more areas that require attention, before we have transferred this entire region to exist and function within His Kingdom reign."

Jennifer nodded. "I understand. We must finish what we've started here for the good of my children and theirs. For the good of all of those who come after them and so forth. Like He says in Deuteronomy 7:9: 'Therefore know that the Lord your God, He is God, the faithful God who keeps covenant and mercy for a thousand generations with those who love Him and keep His commandments.' I believe He will be faithful to all those that come after me because of what You and I are doing right now, obeying His instruction."

"Not only that Jenni, because you have chosen to 'shama,' to listen and follow My instruction and hovering, you will receive the fullness of the promise in Deuteronomy 7:12-15: 'Then it shall come to pass, because you listen to these judgements, and keep and do them, that the LORD your God will keep with you the covenant and the mercy which He swore to your fathers. And He will love you and bless you and multiply you; He will also bless the fruit of your womb and the fruit of your land, your grain and your new wine and your oil, the increase of your cattle and the offspring of your flock, in the land of which He swore to your fathers to give you. You shall be blessed above all peoples; there shall not be a male or female barren among you or among your livestock. And the LORD will take away from you all sickness, and will afflict you with none of the terrible diseases of Egypt which you have known, but will lay them on all who hate you.'" He said as

He placed His finger on the map, over the area that now needed to be cleaned.

The Control Tower

Jennifer took a deep breath and asked, "Holy Spirit, what is the name of this place? Please show me how it functions." She then looked earnestly upon the area His finger was placed on that required 'cleaning.'

"What do you see Jenni?" He quired.

"I see a control tower, built with grey bricks. Mould has grown on the bricks. It's cold… it actually looks like a watch tower for a prison, but it's empty," she described.

"That's right. We cannot leave it here though. It must be demolished to protect your future family line," He advised. *"Go inside and look around."*

As she stepped in, Jennifer noticed that the controls were on but unattended. A dim search light had been left on to scan the area around the tower, going to and fro. She touched a coffee cup sitting next to the control panel. The cup felt warm but as she peered inside it there was only a small amount of coffee in the bottom.

"What are these controls for, Holy Spirit?" she enquired, wondering what kind of 'protection company' held this post, as it looked like they had only recently departed.

"This tower, its controls and the search light, are a part of the self-conservation army that once held this area. The army has now gone, as you can see, in response to the steps you carried out from one to twelve. However, the tower, the controls and the comforts used to maintain its operation remain," He answered.

"I built all this with the opposition?" she asked.

"You did," He replied.

"Imagine what I could build with You then — the real and true creative power."

"We made you, and all of mankind, to be creative like Us, made in Our image. We are creative and unique, hence you, and all of mankind, are filled with this creative power," He explained. Jennifer ran her fingers over the control panel, pondering His words as she peered out of a large observation space in the wall of the tower.

"You've had the ability to create since you were created," He continued, *"We put it in you. We made you like Us, to build and tear down. So for you, anything is possible. Your life on the earth depends only upon who you choose to build and align with. This will be the same for all who proceed you, Jenni. 'See, I have this day set you over nations and over kingdoms, to root out and to pull down, to destroy and to throw down, to build and to plant.*[32]*'"*

"So why did I build this with them? I want to know so I can put a stop to this once and for all. Not just for me, but for all who come after me in my family line," she insisted.

"You built this here with them to prevent the decomposition of your own agenda, to achieve your own end. You watched carefully to assure none would take this land you are preserving" He explained while pointing to the land behind the tower.

She turned around to look at the land He was referring to. Jennifer saw a vast razor wire fence that looked ten feet tall. It surrounded an empty plot of land filled with weeds.

"I built this to protect a field of weeds?" she questioned Him with an element of confusion.

Holy Spirit simply replied *"Yes, you did. To protect your own end, your life. This is the area that you once would not allow Me, or any of Us, to have. Maybe I'm not being clear enough. You didn't want Us to protect you; you wanted to ensure the viability of your life through your own means. Which in doing so, robbed you for a time of your ultimate purpose, and caused you to become a hypocrite as you walked as an enemy to the Cross of Christ. You wanted to be in control of this particular area permanently, not trusting Us to bless you or keep you,"* He added.

"What am I to do now?" Jennifer enquired.

"You must choose to turn the search light off. Turning this light off is the first step you must take to destroy what remains here. It is an act of trust in Me; in Us and Our protection of you," He informed her.

She looked at the control panel in front of her and flicked the search light switch to the off position. The whole area went dark. The coolness of the tower began to seep into her beautiful garment. But as it did, she remembered she had not asked Him the question: "Holy Spirit, where did this all begin?"

As the words left her mouth, a light appeared from within her heart, flickering strongly and dispersing the darkness.

"Look into the light Jenni. It is illuminating the core," He advised. She looked into the flickering light and she recognised an injustice issue. For the first time she was able to understand why she had self-conservation wounds in her heart; she was able to clearly see the link. She now wanted justice for the pain that caused this wound — significant justice! She was intrigued by her own heart. Her inner most being was beginning to pull to Him and His Justice. She no longer shied away or wanted to run from scenarios. Jennifer wanted what she was here for — His Justice for the pain that led to the wound!

She suddenly started to experience pain in her left hip. Holy Spirit imparted His wisdom to her and she recognised that she was carrying the pain of self-conservation in her hip. Jennifer then understood that self-conservation affected her walk, and made bearing healthy, whole, spiritual fruit near impossible.

Jennifer remembered dreaming as a child of having a dog to keep her company in her room because she had a great fear of the dark and what lurked within it.

Immediately, a sharp ring manifested in her left ear, "Augh!" she cried clutching her ear. What seemed easy a moment ago began to feel uncomfortable as a storm brewed internally. This storm produced a sharp headache in the middle of her forehead.

The Little Girl

She carefully began to look into her heart and was met by the sound of a little girl singing whilst playing with her doll. All of a sudden, she saw a demon appear next to the little girl. The little girl was unaware of its proximity to her as she continued to play in her beautiful white dress printed with dainty blue flowers. Jennifer then saw a gremlin and a picture of a demonic face from a movie, then another and another... a creepy man wearing a hockey mask with a chainsaw. Jennifer's heart was pulled to and fro by the pictures that were stored within it from the horror movies she had willingly watched in her life. These pictures began to fight against her, in an attempt to induce an inconsolable state of fear. To hold her in a place where she would be impotent and unable to rule.

Nevertheless, Jennifer persisted in her course of action, knowing that she was not alone — Holy Spirit was **with** her.

Jennifer then recalled wanting to sleep with the light on whilst growing up because it enabled her to constantly assess the safety of her environment. Her heart believed an attack was imminent because it housed ungodly rocks from watching horror movies. Every time the eyes of her heart looked within to see if the threat was real, they saw the ungodly rocks, which confirmed the need for her to remain on constant alert. Jennifer was afraid of being robbed, harmed or killed; hence she watched and watched to prevent these events taking place. She became a person on guard, in control, ruling out every possibility day and night.

She then saw herself waking up in the night in a state of fright! She quickly assessed the scenario; her room was lit by the hallway light. Jennifer was exhausted; she knew she could not keep watch anymore.

The Redemption

With tears flowing from her eyes, she took courage and whispered, "Where are You Jesus? Where are You? I'm scared! I need You."

"I'm right here Jenni," Jesus replied. He did not tell her it was only a dream or to go back to sleep, He knew it was real. He knew she was under attack and needed His help. He crouched down next to her bed and lovingly stroked her hair, wet and tangled from her tears of distress. Jennifer looked into His eyes and started to feel safe.

"Jenni, would you like to come with Me?" Jesus asked her.

"Yes, I can't stay here anymore, not like this, not ever. I don't want to be here." She wrapped her arms around His shoulders. Jennifer knew Jesus understood demons were real and that she was under attack, in need of His protection. As she wiped the tears from her cheeks and looked up, she noticed there were no more demons. Her room was empty and had been newly fitted with a bright white staircase to Heaven, belonging to Him. Relief, peace and love expanded in her heart. She then took His hand to journey with Him to His Heavenly Kingdom.

As her foot touched the first step, she noticed that her nightgown had changed, it was now glowing white. She was then greeted by a mighty angel, and as she looked upward, she saw multitudes of them all the way along the staircase. They were armed not with weapons, but with song! Jennifer knew that no force from hell could penetrate their praise, and a deep rest presented within her. She now understood that He had assigned angels to her, to the staircase she would use all the days of her life.

When Jesus and Jennifer entered Heaven, He opened a white door and directed her to go through it, into a room full of armour. Not just any armour, but armour that appeared extra strong, extra sturdy, reliable and true. The armour looked as if it was alive and impenetrable. She looked at Jesus curiously and said, "It looks like it's for me? It looks like it would fit me perfectly." Jennifer ran her fingers across its form.

Jesus smiled at her. *"It's time to put it on Jenni,"* He said as He held up the breast plate of righteousness in front of her.

She placed each piece of her armour on with His help — the breast plate, the belt, the shoes, the helmet, the sword and the shield — realising that as long as she was wearing it, she would be just fine because He empowered it all.

She looked at the armour on her body. "It fits like a glove… where's all this light coming from though? It wasn't lit up in this way when I first saw it in the room," she remarked, pointing to the flicking and flashing that seemed to be imbedded within its structure. "See, look at it."

Jesus laughed. *"Jenni, that light is coming from your heart. The Kingdom of God within you gives your armour its light. Your heart determines its effectiveness,"* He instructed.

"Oh," she paused. "My heart is doing this… it's incredible."

"No Jenni, not incredible — it's the Kingdom. It is Father God, the Holy Spirit and I, living and active within you, penetrating and piercing the world around you. To build up and tear down, when and wherever required. As long as you remain in Me and I in you, you will be protected. You have no need to fear, to trade or to look elsewhere for protection, you have it already. You only need to engage with My Justice. It's that simple," He replied.

"In My name giants will fall, every knee must bow and every enemy must

flee. You are free to live a life for Me, and fulfil your scroll, without any fear of harm from the enemy."

The Wisdom

Jennifer brushed her hands along the breastplate of righteousness she now wore, which glowed with Kingdom light.

Holy Spirit pointed to the map of her heart. *"Look now Jenni, what do you see?"* He asked as He circled the area with His finger that they had just 'mopped up.'

"I see a meadow filled with fruit trees. I see blossoms ready to bring forth fruit full of His sweetness and life to heal the nations," she stated.

"You have left self-conservation behind. The inside of your cup, your heart, is clean. Your heart blooms with His Justice which fuels the Kingdom of God within you, protecting you and guiding you" He confirmed.

Chapter Fourteen

♥

Step Fourteen: Self-congestion

Distancing from God's abundance

Jennifer started to hear the chatter and noises of a school yard during lunch time. "Why am I already receiving this intel Holy Spirit? I haven't even been standing on this step for a minute."

"The acceleration process has given you great sensitivity to the spirit realm. Hence, you are already sensing what needs to be dealt with in this place. With this increase comes a great responsibility," He remarked. *"You will be required to uphold the law."*

"What do you mean? I thought Christ came so I didn't have to uphold the law? That doesn't sound right to me at all Holy Spirit," she questioned Him.

"You will be required to bring every part of your heart that is hovered over by Me, to Him for reconciliation to ensure it is filled with His justice," He explained.

She began to mull over what He had just said. "So, when I begin to hear and see, I need to recognise it is You directing me to an area needing justice."

"Yes, that's right — His Justice is the fulfilment of the law," Holy Spirit confirmed as He kissed her on the forehead.

"But what if I don't respond straight away? Or what if I get it wrong?" she queried.

"You can't get it wrong Jenni. And if your response is delayed, don't worry, I will keep hovering over your heart until it is reconciled. This is the prerogative of our God, your God and Mine," He answered.

"That's a relief! Where are we then? I take it we are in a school yard?" she probed.

The Light on the Map

Holy Spirit presented the map of her heart before them, and as He unrolled it light shone from it. "My goodness, what is that?" she asked, shielding her eyes from the penetrating light.

"That is the light shining from your heart! Remember the map reflects your

heart position," He reminded her, smiling like a proud teacher looking upon His student.

"It's never done this before! I DO have a different heart now; I have His Justice in me!" she stated in awe.

Jennifer looked to the Heavens above, closed her eyes, and took a moment. She then whispered to Father God, from her innermost being: "Thank You Papa, thank You for saving me and bringing me here. Thank You for transforming me." Soft tears of joy rolled down her cheeks.

"Now, your map, My darling," Holy Spirit said, guiding her focus back to the task at hand.

The Apex of the Heart

"We are here. We have 'mopped up' here, but now we must attend to this area…" He stated, pointing to the areas of light, then to a darkened area that looked to be near the tip of her heart. *"This area is of primary importance, Jenni."* Holy Spirit added with a serious tone.

"The apex is responsible for keeping your heart moving forward with Us, to build and expand. It enables you to keep handing over the evil to Him with JOY for His redemption. Confidently knowing you will be rightfully reinstated with Father God, and thus facilitate the transfer of Mount Zion's authority to earth. 'Those who trust in the LORD are like Mount Zion, which cannot be moved, but abides forever. As the mountains surround Jerusalem, so the LORD surrounds His people from this time forth and forever.[33]*' We must make sure this area is swept clean of any debris and entities that seek to stop your heart moving forward. There is an agreement here, one that has inhibited the function of your heart's apex"* He informed her. *"Look at this area of your heart Jenni, what do you see?"*

The Black Tar

"I see black, sticky tar. It sticks to my feet. I can't get it off no matter how hard I try," she calmly described.

"What else is the tar doing Jenni, besides sticking to your feet?" He asked coaching her along. Jennifer looked deeper into the picture.

"It's moving up my legs, like branches, crawling higher and higher up my body… it's coming up my neck… oh my goodness! It's heading toward my mouth!!!!" she screamed as panic rose in her heart. She became so distressed that she started to experience sharp stomach pains.

She took a deep breath in and out, then closed her eyes to connect with the eyes of her heart. Jennifer saw them looking at what remained of the ungodly rock pile, then she began to challenge the eyes of her heart to take another look: "What can you see? Can you see the expanse of His Kingdom in you?" She watched as the eyes of her heart quickly redirected to His Kingdom within it, away from the diminishing rock pile.

Jennifer regained her strength and courage, and then the words she needed left her mouth: "Holy Spirit, where did this all begin?"

Suddenly, she saw something she was not expecting. "Augh!" she called out in despair, as the pain sharpened in her stomach.

"Remember Jenni, this is the type of fasting He requires — rend your heart before Him. 'Now, therefore, says the LORD, turn to Me with all your heart, with fasting, with weeping, and with mourning. So rend your heart, and not your garments; return to the LORD your God, for He is gracious and merciful, slow to anger, and of great kindness; and He relents from doing harm.[34]" Holy Spirit decreed.

The Prayer to the Ungodly

Bravely determined, she looked again at the scenario Holy Spirit presented to her, responsible for the tar, the agreement and the pain. She could see herself at her parents' house as a teen in her bed, praying. Not just praying, but begging God in absolute distress, not to make her fat! She watched on with tears. Then she saw a cold shiver enter her younger self as she laid out her request: "If I have to choose, please don't make me fat. I'll be happy with pimples, just don't make me fat."

Young Jennifer did not know what to do with the pain of being bullied at school. All she could see was that being thin would mean she would be accepted and successful. Jennifer now understood that her younger self had ascertained that she could cover up the pimples with make-up and hence live with them, because 'fatness' could not be covered up! To the younger desperate Jennifer, making a deal with 'god' seemed like a win-win scenario; He could make the bullying stop if she made a deal with Him.

Jennifer watched as this scared young teen acted on the lie she believed — that Father God was a god of punishment, whom she could at best only hope to bargain with.

"You were manipulated by the enemy. It was never Father God you were 'praying' to, it was a demon disguised, manipulating you to create further distress in your life. This demon kept you locked in and under its control. In this cycle, you lost the ability to be strong and courageous, the ability to finish things well, the ability to rely on Us and to pull on Us successfully. We ARE life Jenni; there is nothing without Us" He explained to her.

The Redemption

Jennifer suddenly saw the LORD Jesus stretch out His hand to her, she did not even have to ask the question, "Where are You Jesus?" She now knew He was there waiting, wanting to pull her out, and understood that grasping His hand would free her. A smile from deep within Jennifer rose up, as her eyes gazed upon the beauty of Christ. She then stretched forth her right hand toward

His. When His hand touched hers, she simply lifted her right leg, followed by her left, and she was released from the entrapment of the deadly cycle. No black, sticky tar was able to restrain her anymore.

"LORD," Jennifer whispered in Jesus' ear as she wrapped her arms around Him, delighting in Him with every fibre of her being.

"LORD," she professed again from her heart. She felt Him smile. Jennifer pressed her chest against His and a divine exchange took place from this embrace. The Kingdom of God within her heart started to move to and fro freely within Him, and He within her heart. An anointing came upon her heavily, unlike anything she had ever experienced before. She was free. His face was clearer to her now than it had ever been. She could see His hair, His beard, His facial features, His eyes. His gentle bluish-green eyes. Jennifer could see Him as He is.

He held her face in His hands and stroked her cheek with His thumb and spoke to her heart. *"Fear not, for I am with you; be not dismayed, for I am your God. I will strengthen you, yes, I will help you, I will uphold you with My righteous right hand.*[35]*"*

The Wisdom

Jennifer inhaled His peace, which seemed to saturate her heart with His river of life and a liquid gold-type substance.

"This gold, Holy Spirit, that is within my heart, can you please tell me about it? It is beautiful," she asked.

"To put it simply, the gold is the Kingdom within you. Gold in the heart exists where the divine nature of Father God abides, where His Justice rests. The gold areas are where He is made manifest in your heart. The liquid gold is poured in to build upon His foundation of righteousness, to form walls, buildings, streets, runways... His city, His Kingdom," He explained.

"It is written in Ezekiel 36:26-28: 'I will give you a new heart and put a new spirit within you; I will take the heart of stone out of your flesh and give you a heart of flesh. I will put My Spirit within you and cause you to walk in My statutes, and you will keep My judgements and do them. Then you shall dwell in the land that I gave to your fathers; you shall be My people, and I will be your God.'"

"The heart of flesh is the heart of nakedness, filled with Him and His Justice. Returning it to the place of Eden, walking freely with God in the garden, in a state of nakedness where there is nothing to separate you from Him, nothing to hide, as it was before the fall."

"So yes, a consecrated heart, is a heart that has the river of life, His garden of Eden, and Kingdom of gold within it. There is also another piece of wisdom you must acquire from this scripture in Ezekiel," He added, patiently waiting for her to ask the right question.

Jennifer looked at the map of her heart and focused on the scripture, and replied, "It's the stone, the heart of stone, isn't it? This map, the map of my heart, did not have light when we first began. I did not have power fuelled armour, and I certainly didn't have gold in my heart. I had stone, a large ungodly rock pile! What is the significance of this stone, Holy Spirit?" she answered, hoping she had presented the correct question to Him.

Holy Spirit smiled. *"The stone is magnetic."*

"Magnetic?" she replied, astounded by His response, wondering what magnetism could possibly have to do with ungodly rocks in a person's heart.

"Yes Jenni, rock is magnetic. Mankind mine the rocks and minerals of the earth which are filled with magnetic substances like iron, nickel and cobalt. The earth is surrounded by a magnetic field, creating a magnetic force all around it. So why do you think it is so important to Us to remove the parts in the heart that are made of ungodly rock?" Holy Spirit asked her, prodding her heart for an answer.

"So… the magnetic field outside the earth does not draw or pull on the heart, I guess?" she replied.

"Yes, that's right Jenni, that's absolutely right! The heart of ungodly rock is what connects a person to the principalities and powers above the earth. You will recall this from Ephesians 6:12: 'For we do not wrestle against flesh and blood, but against principalities, against powers, against the rulers of the darkness of this age, against the spiritual hosts of wickedness in the heavenly places.' This is very important to remember." He stated to clarify His explanation.

"Yes! I get it! When the heart of stone, the 'rocks' are removed, connections are severed with the spiritual forces of evil in the heavenly places! There is no drawing out, no magnetism where His Kingdom is, because magnets don't stick to gold, right? A soft heart, a heart of gold, is in the secret place and cannot be drawn out by a magnetic force!" Jennifer elated.

"That's right, magnets do not stick to gold because gold is naturally non-magnetic. Gold actually repels a strong magnetic field. And if a magnet looks like it is sticking to gold, that is because the gold is not pure and harbours contaminates. These contaminates are the magnetic elements, which represent the ungodly agreements, trades, oaths and contracts that are connected to the magnetic forces outside the earth — the principalities and powers!" He recapped.

"I get it… Jesus came to give us His Justice, so we could once again abide with Him in Eden. It was literally the only way back for us! A heart of stone, the rocks, draw us out and join us to the spiritual forces of evil in the heavenly places, whereas a heart of gold is joined to Father God's throne and is naturally repelled by this ungodly magnetism. A heart of gold is only found in Mount Zion, with our Father!" she exclaimed.

"What else does He say about gold?" Holy Spirit enquired.

She ran through the scriptures in her heart and presented what she found to Holy Spirit — "'All the gold is Mine!' Yes! This is written in Haggai 2:8: 'The silver is Mine, and the gold is Mine, says the LORD of hosts.' He wants back what is rightfully His — the human heart in its original created state, like it was before we were sent here. Which is only possible through Christ's righteousness, the silver!" Jennifer answered Him excitedly.

"That's right Jenni, you have a listening ear! I am the wise reprover, I am the One, sent by the LORD who leads people to obtain a heart of gold; a heart filled with His Justice, His Kingdom, His river of life. I have in Me the seven Spirits of God that facilitate this to take place. 'Like an earring of gold and an ornament of fine gold is a wise rebuker to an obedient ear.[36]*"*

Jennifer exhaled deeply with a smile that extended from the very tip of her heart. "Thank You Holy Spirit, I could never have done any of this without You."

Step Fifteen: Self-service

Declining the invitation to submit and trust

Jennifer directed her gaze gently upward to what lay before her — the broad place, the throne the LORD had appointed to her upon her mountain. It was a gift, assigned to her from when Father God created her before the beginning of time. Until climbing this staircase with Holy Spirit, she had no idea that this mountain even existed or that it held a seat divinely created for her.

A gentle breeze wrapped around her, and she tangibly felt the call to immediate increase.

Holy Spirit tucked her wavy, thick hair behind her ears. *"This one is going to give you access to your gate at the base of your mountain. As you open your gate and complete this acceleration journey, you will open gates for others to help them navigate through the wilderness of their own lives,"* He outlined.

She pondered His words, "So I can fulfil the invitation... His purpose for me?"

"Exactly. He is ready and willing to help you fulfil every word He has spoken. His Justice will set you and your gate free. This is the simplicity of the Kingdom — everything is of Him and in Him. 'For of Him and through Him and to Him are all things, to whom be the glory forever. Amen.[37]*'"* Holy Spirit decreed.

Living Psalm 91

"You are now living out the reality of Psalm 91 Jenni. 'In their hands they shall bear you up, lest thou dash your foot against a stone. You shall tread upon the lion and the cobra, the young lion and the serpent you shall trample underfoot. Because he has set his love upon Me, therefore I will deliver him; I will set him on high, because he has known My name. He shall call upon Me, and I will answer him; I will be with him in trouble; I will deliver him and honor him. With long life I will satisfy him, and show him My salvation.[38]*'"*

"The 'stone' mentioned here, which We keep you from harming yourself

on, refers to the consequences of building on the 'ungodly rock pile.' Remember, you were designed to build and create just like Us. Instead of being destroyed by building on the rock pile, with Us you remove the ungodly things that have deceived you through trades, agreements, oaths and contracts. Which enables you to set your love upon Him and trust Him, through His Justice, hence He delivers you when you call upon Him," Holy Spirit explained.

"I'm in the secret place! Just like it says in Psalm 91:1-2: 'He who dwells in the secret place of the Most High shall abide under the shadow of the Almighty. I will say of the LORD, He is my refuge and my fortress; my God, in Him I will trust.' All that You and I have been doing with the LORD, has transferred me here, to the secret place with our Father, in His protection and provision!" she exclaimed.

"Exactly! Now, let's take a look at conquering this gate," He invited her.

Jennifer's eyes followed His finger to the area on the map where her gate lay. *"This is all we need to conquer now for you to begin to rule and reign in your life from your mountain. The gate rests here at the bottom, we will take this back first. There is a strong opposition here that would prefer you not to take this gate — focus on Me is key, Jenni."* He instructed.

The Web

"What do you see Jenni?" She started to travel through a mass of dark grey clouds. She saw two people exchange what looked like money for some documents in a brief case. Then, they went their separate ways. As they went, she saw what looked like a spider web joining them together. Jennifer touched the spider web with her right pointer finger out of sheer curiosity, and as she did, it twanged like a guitar string and gave her an unfriendly jolt. "What was that?"

"That Jenni, is an exchange... a trade. This trade has bound the two people together; no matter what they do or where they go, they are bound to each other," He outlined.

"Does it ever break?" she asked. *"No Jenni, it cannot be broken by the human hand or pressure or even death. It always remains"* He answered.

"What do You mean death cannot break it?" she questioned Him.

"The death of one human connected to the other bound by trade does not destroy the trade agreement. It still exists when one of the involved parties dies, or even if both parties die and leave the physical earth. The trade agreement continues to exist and affects the family line of the people connected to it," He added.

"It can be destroyed by the Blood right? And the power in His name?" Jennifer enquired confidently.

"Yes Jenni, it can. It is written in Revelation 12:11: 'And they overcame him by the blood of the Lamb and by the word of their testimony, and they did not love their lives to the death.' And in Acts 4:12: 'Nor is there salvation in any other,

for there is no other name under heaven given among men by which we must be saved.'" He declared.

"Look again Jenni," He advised her. Jennifer looked closely as Holy Spirit pulled the scenario forward in her heart. She was then able to clearly see and hear the interaction between the two people. She saw that the exchange was made between a man and a woman in an abandoned industrial area that was cold and damp — a place where mildew freely grew.

The woman in the trade wore a black trench coat and had a black brief case in her left hand. The man in the trade had a handful of money. Jennifer knew the money had value for certain things, but was limited, because it was foreign currency.

"Oh, he's ripping her off! That money in his hand has limits," she alerted Holy Spirit.

"Keep looking Jenni," He coached her.

Jennifer noticed that there was something quite strange and odd about the man talking to the woman. He wore a dated, grey suit, with a thick, grey tie. He had old fashioned glasses and one of his shoes had a hole in the toe, with a toenail sticking out of it. Jennifer kept looking and listening.

She then heard the woman say: "I don't trust Him to give me what I desire or want, but you say you can give me what I want now?" The man in the grey suit replied to her question with confidence. "I can. I will give you these finances so you can have what you desire right now. You will have what you want. You just need to give me your constitution and that's all it will cost you. I will see to it that your every desire and want is met, which is written upon its pages."

The woman smiled, but her smile was somewhat filled with evil intent as she handed him the brief case. She then snatched the finances out of the hand of the man in the grey suit.

"You're quite desperate for this, aren't you?" the man said smiling. He admired the woman's hastiness; her desperation to make this trade with him. Jennifer could see that this man enjoyed the deal on an innate spiritual level.

"I don't want anything holding me back anymore. I want what I want," she replied with a cold obstinance, then turned and walked away. The man in the grey suit laughed as he rubbed the black suit case with his scaly, old hands which now appeared to have very dirty claws instead of fingernails.

"Foolish human, foolish," he said as he walked away with the brief case.

"HUH," Jennifer breathed in deeply. "She has just made a deal with an evil spirit!" she announced, looking at Holy Spirit troubled by all she had seen and heard.

"No Jenni, she has made a deal with the devil," He corrected her.

"What are You going to do about it?" Jennifer asked Holy Spirit, awaiting His crucial strategy to free the woman.

He looked at her lovingly *"Jenni, this is your jurisdiction now. You are in the*

LORD, and He in you. This is where you start functioning as a king and a priest. The correct question is, 'what are YOU going to do about it?' Fulfil your calling Jenni, choose it," He corrected her as He pointed to the gate that led to the throne on top of her mountain. *"This position is yours. If you do not take it, no one ever will. It is yours. The devil will keep doing what he's doing to your family line on your watch if you choose not to take your rightful place to rule and reign with the LORD,"* Holy Spirit informed her.

Jennifer took a deep breath in and exhaled to focus. Closing her eyes, she regained perspective and started to speak to her heart. "I am a king and priest on this earth. You 'have made us kings and priests to our God; and we shall reign on the earth.[39]' You have made me!" He quickened her heart and she asked, "Holy Spirit, what is this trade called?"

The Fifteenth Law

Smiling, He replied to her *"Self-service. It is one of the most common trades. One chooses not to trust the Word and avoids doing the required heart work with Me, and thus ends up bound to the enemy. This way, personal justice systems are fulfilled, which cause people to always look for new agreements and trade opportunities. This is a common block for most people. It stops them from taking their gate and hence their mountain. You cannot function as a king or priest without trust in Him"* Holy Spirit reminded her.

"Did I inherit this, Holy Spirit? The woman... it wasn't 'me,'" she queried.

"Yes, you did. It has held your gate captive over your life time," He said raising His eyebrows.

The Sunday School Picnic

Jennifer began to see her younger self, and other children playing at a Sunday School picnic. She had decided to go swimming with her friends that day in the river. Other kids were swimming and there were adults standing by. All was well. She was so happy to charge into the water with the others in her swimwear!

There was splashing and playing, diving and handstands. Jennifer and a few other children including her best bud at the time, Adam, decided to play 'ring-a-ring-a-rosy' in the river.

Jennifer smiled as she looked at the vision, but as she did, a force began to pull at her feet. She looked down at the fifteenth step she stood on, but could not see what had pulled at her. She then continued to watch the children in the vision. They all sang loudly and bobbed up and down to the rhyme.

Suddenly, Jennifer began to panic. "I don't think I can watch anymore Holy Spirit" she said, putting both of her hands over her mouth to control her breathing. "I..."

"Jenni, I'm right here, the same as always." He rubbed her back and

whispered in her ear. *"You can do this."*

Jennifer re-engaged, and there it was, the pull! She was pulled under and struggled to the surface, only to be pulled under again! Jennifer could scream only momentarily as she was pulled again and again by a rip in the river. She was drowning!

Adam, her best bud, was in the same predicament! Jennifer could see two children drowning in the river, and **knew** one of them was her!

"My chest Holy Spirit, my chest, I can't breathe!" Jennifer screamed, clutching her chest, feeling like she was having a heart attack.

Adam's Dad

"Keep looking Jenni, He's coming" Holy Spirit reassured her. Then there was a great commotion in the water as Adam's dad came to rescue them.

He was a tall, strong man and had no regard for his own life, only the life of his son and his friends. He picked both Jennifer and Adam up in his arms and took them to the bank of the river. Frightened, the two children shook and quivered, despite towels being wrapped around them and reassurance given by their parents.

"That was the trigger that activated the self-service trade in your heart. You were too afraid to venture back in, in case you lost your footing again, so you found another way," Holy Spirit explained.

Jennifer began to weep. "But where was He when I was drowning? I don't understand?" she asked, needing an answer to reconcile her heart.

The Redemption

With a deep breath she turned her heart back to the scenario filled with pain and doubt. Her quivering voice then released the question that would bring godly resolve once and for all, "Where were You, Jesus?" For the first time she saw Him there, right there before the pull began. He was, in fact, right next to her, smiling and enjoying the fun too. Then as Jennifer felt the first tug from below by the spider web that connected her to the trade in her family line, she called loudly to Him, "Jesus!!"

Jennifer released His name again with all that was of Him in her heart as the water began to overwhelm her. "Jesus!!" She instantly felt His right arm wrap around her and then saw His strong-arm grasp Adam. All the pulling stopped. She caught her breath, so did Adam. Both children wiped the water from their eyes. *"Come on,"* He smiled at them both, kissing each of them on the head.

With a child on each hip, Jesus carried them up the white staircase, which to little Jennifer and Adam seemed to be suspended above the water.

Jennifer rested her head upon His shoulder, tired from what had just happened. At the top of the staircase, Jesus popped Jennifer and Adam down onto the solid floor of crystal waters. Both the children looked at it and realised it would not give way, and knew they were completely safe. Jennifer took another deep breath in and out, and started to admire the surroundings. She saw angels and noticed that both she and Adam were no longer in swimwear but in lovely white gowns, the brightest white she had ever seen.

Jennifer liked her gown. She swayed to the gentle angelic worship that surrounded them. Jesus started to walk Jennifer and Adam toward the throne. The children **knew** Who they were walking towards and then ran to the throne. "Papa!" the children squealed excitedly.

Father God opened His arms wide to embrace them both, and said with great joy, *"Jenni, Adam."* The children sat on His knee upon the throne, kicking their little legs and smiling, enjoying all the attention He had to give them.

Father God gently tucked Jennifer's cleansed hair behind her ears, and asked her, *"Do you think you can trust me to keep your feet secure? Then you can delight in what I place in your heart."*

"Yes, I can," she confidently answered as she kissed Father God on His cheek.

The Wisdom

"Holy Spirit, the near-drowning in the river with Adam and I... the trade the woman made... it all reflects what's been happening from the very beginning, doesn't it? The same enemy as in the beginning has lied to us, deceived us, and tried to destroy us. Then the LORD Jesus came and rescued us. He did, the LORD Jesus did! This is incredible! He has the power to free us from all trades, from all ungodly things. And then He presents us perfected by His Blood, redeemed, before the throne of Father God as His rescued children," she recapped to Holy Spirit from what she had just experienced firsthand.

"Indeed, He does Jenni. Now take a look at your gate. What do you see?" He enquired.

"I see a large frame of gold covered in a flowering green vine. I see a vast green meadow with children playing, and His river of life running through it, surrounded by His light," she described. "It is beautiful! Thank You Holy Spirit for leading me," Jennifer whispered as she pressed into His chest.

"You're welcome Jenni. You are a king and priest to our God. Reconciling what is His back to Him through His Justice, giving Him His full reward," He congratulated her.

"My goodness, this is so intense and incredible all at once," Jennifer stated, looking joyfully at Holy Spirit. "I feel so free," she said, overjoyed, as she squeezed her face between her hands.

Holy Spirit laughed and nodded in agreement.

Chapter Sixteen

Step Sixteen: Self-ruination

Denial of the completeness of God

"'In the beginning was the Word, and the Word was with God, and the Word was God. He was in the beginning with God. All things were made through Him, and without Him nothing was made that was made. In Him was life, and the life was the light of men. And the light shines in the darkness, and the darkness did not comprehend it.[40]' Do you understand this scripture, Jenni?" Holy Spirit asked as He gently held Jennifer's right hand between His. She opened her eyes and smiled as her gaze met His, "I do Holy Spirit."

He grinned and enquired, *"What do you see?"*

"I see myself standing with the LORD on a high place, a very high place. Surrounded by the sound of worshipping angels," she answered as her thick, shiny hair danced in the warm breeze.

"I am on my mountain with my Father."

"Yes, you are. Do you recognise the time?" Holy Spirit questioned her, enquiring of her heart.

"It is before I was sent here to earth, when Father God created me. I see Him discussing with me my mission upon the earth. We are reasoning together at the top of my mountain," she gently replied.

"It's time to take back what He, what We, assigned to you in the beginning. He made this mountain for you and assigned His life force to it. Once you obtain it, it all will be activated. He is faithful Jenni, have no doubt, this will come to pass. This is His plan and has been from the very beginning; that His children rule and reign on the mountains He has assigned to them," Holy Spirit stated as He tucked her hair behind her ears.

Tucking of the Hair

Jennifer rested her hand gently upon His and asked, "Holy Spirit, why do You always tuck my hair behind my ears?"

A broad smile appeared on His face, *"Because My dear, the glory of the*

LORD increases upon you as you accelerate. Your hair manifests His glory, so I simply tuck it behind your ears so you can see."

"Jenni," He added, *"I have some wisdom for you: this is not the end! This is the beginning of your journey, ruling and reigning in the land We assigned to you."*

Jennifer smiled, "I'm so grateful this is only the beginning! I now know that I have nowhere else to go — but with the LORD! Just like the twelve disciples said to Jesus: 'Lord, to whom shall we go? You have the words of eternal life. Also we have come to believe and know that You are the Christ, the Son of the living God.' No turning back for me now" she replied.

He nodded, *"That's right Jenni, no turning back! Your heart has won this battle of love with His Justice and it KNOWS it! So now this will be how you function; according to the original design of your heart. Your heart will transfer the Kingdom through your soul, your mind and then your body. This is what I like to call 'homeostasis.' From now on, no matter what your physical body presents to your heart, your heart will feed back Kingdom truth through your soul and mind, to your body. You will live from the Kingdom of God, the river of life. You will experience incredible transformation within your physical body, Jenni, because of this. Your heart has chosen well!"* Holy Spirit explained to her.

"I really get it now. When Jesus walked the earth fully man and fully God in a physical body, He endured the beatings, the pulling of His beard, the lashings, the crown of thorns and the agony of crucifixion. Yet when the pain was sent from His body to His heart, it was shut down by the Kingdom of God filling His heart! He loved God with all His heart, because He knew He was and is the Son of God! This is why we cannot love Him when we use our own fraudulent justice systems, only when we embrace His Justice in our hearts. It takes God to love God!" she stated.

"Yes! Your heart knows you are a daughter of God because you have built with Us, establishing His Kingdom within it. Now, when your body presents information to your heart such as 'you are this or that, I am sick or I am hurt,' your heart will not give life to this script as it did before. The eyes of your heart will look around to see if this information is true. And as the eyes of your heart look around, they will see His Kingdom established, His garden of Eden, the river of life, and the city you have built with Him within it. Then your heart will know to abolish all opposing information and will continue on with Kingdom function. You will find you won't experience sickness and disease the way you used to. You will find your emotions to be stable. You will see His promises fulfilled as they have somewhere to land — the airport within His Kingdom city in your heart," He added.

"I know that my heart, soul, mind and body will not go back now, as His Kingdom governs my heart. Holy Spirit... that's why Jesus was never sick on the earth isn't it? That's why Jesus never lacked power on the earth, right? He loved God with His whole heart because He was and is God. His heart KNEW who He was!" she probed.

"When Jesus walked the earth, fully man and fully God, His heart was (and is) perfect. Any sickness or disease that was presented to His body was instantly shut down by His heart. Sickness and disease cannot penetrate His Kingdom. This is written in Revelation 21:4–5: 'And God will wipe away every tear from their eyes; there shall be no more death, nor sorrow, nor crying. There shall be no more pain, for the former things have passed away. Then He who sat on the throne said, behold, I make all things new. And He said to me, write, for these words are true and faithful.' It is impossible for His Kingdom to harbour death, sorrow, pain or to lack power. His Kingdom makes all things new. His Kingdom is eternal, it builds and it establishes. This is written in Isaiah 9:7: 'Of the increase of His government and peace there will be no end, upon the throne of David and over His kingdom, to order it and establish it with judgement and justice from that time forward, even forever. The zeal of the LORD of hosts will perform this.'"

There was a reverential silence between them as Jennifer pondered the Word Holy Spirit had just spoken.

The Final Map Presentation

Holy Spirit presented the map pertaining to the region they had conquered together for the last time. After this, the map would no longer be required.

Light from the map illuminated the sixteenth step she stood on. "This has never happened before?" she said surprised as she looked at the light beneath her feet.

"It is your heart connection to your mountain beginning to manifest on the earth. You will see more, much more Jenni, once we address this final area on the map" Holy Spirit explained.

The Cyclone

"Now, look at your mountain, what do you see?" He enquired, placing His right hand over her heart.

As she looked, Jennifer saw a vast cyclone over the top of it with a great darkness in its centre. "What does this mean Holy Spirit? It's eery and unpleasant," she answered.

"I need you to look closer and to be patient. You will receive the answer," He said, requesting her to persist.

Jennifer looked deeper into the blackness of the cyclone. She could see things in the middle of the blackness that resembled particles. Then, by faith, she took her right hand and placed it into the middle of the blackness to grasp a large particle. She pulled her hand out of the blackness tightly holding onto what she had grasped — a huge locust!

"This thing is massive! There must be hundreds, if not thousands of them in there!" she exclaimed, dropping it onto the sixteenth step she stood on and immediately crushing it with her right foot.

"Is there anything else?" He enquired, continuing to prompt her.

She looked back at the cyclone. Jennifer reflected on its rotation; it was going in an anti-clock wise direction. "Oh, I see... this cyclone is robbing me of time! It is stopping me from ruling and reigning over time with the LORD, with my Father! This cyclone is responsible for all the delay of my scroll!" she exclaimed in shock, putting her hands over her mouth. "How long have I let this go on for, Holy Spirit? This is ridiculous!"

Suddenly Jennifer began to lose control, "What's going on Holy Spirit? I feel really dizzy, like I'm going to faint and my breath is feeling tight. I think I'm going to..." she said as her voice faded to below a whisper. Jennifer's body became floppy, her eyes involuntarily closed. She was unable to stand.

"Jenni!" Holy Spirit yelled to get her attention. He quickly placed His hands around her torso to stop her from falling down the staircase she had just climbed. *"Jenni! Don't engage with it,"* He begged her in a loud voice.

Jennifer spontaneously opened her eyes and inhaled deeply, as if she had been given a breath of life. She refocused on His face. *"This is what has robbed you of your rightful place. It has kept you here for far too long, it has tried to destroy everything We sent you to do here upon the earth. It is time for you to destroy it. Enough is enough!"* He proclaimed.

She exhaled forcefully and reconnected with His eyes. She noticed His eyebrows were raised and then knew she was in the framework of His protection and provision, not out on her own. Immediately Jennifer regained her ability to stand firm. She was ready to wage war upon the evil.

"I see a message, a script amongst the winds Holy Spirit," she stated loudly, knowing that when she called out what she saw in the darkness, it lost its power because it was exposed. "I think I can read it... hang on, I'm going to grab the script," she said as she reached her right hand into the cyclone once again. She retrieved the document and handed it to Holy Spirit. "What does it say?" she asked Him.

"Jenni, I am here to teach you, to impart wisdom, knowledge, counsel, might and power to you. You, my dear, must read the script" He explained.

"Oh" she responded, taking the script back in her hands. "I can't see anything on it... that's strange. I saw writing all over it when it was in the midst of the cyclone, but now?"

"That's because in your hand it has the ability to hide. That is part of the trade agreement," He taught her.

Holy Spirit touched the paper and the script started to reappear. She noticed that the writing was written in blood. Jennifer swallowed deeply and began to read aloud what she could. "Self-ruination, permission granted to destroy the physical temple, unable to possess, withheld, protecting self from being parented by Father God..." Jennifer was astounded with what she read.

"When did this happen? Did I really agree to this?" She looked intently at Holy Spirit for an answer.

"You did My dear girl, unknowingly. The enemy will do whatever it takes to prevent the LORD's anointed taking their rightful place. All bets are off with him. He stops at nothing and hides it well from all he deceives. That's why it's called deception. Remember Jenni — people don't realise they are being deceived, because if they did, they wouldn't be deceived now, would they?" He reminded her.

"I guess not. Where did this begin? This self-ruination," she asked.

The Werewolf

Jennifer then heard a child singing. She saw a little girl collecting flowers in a meadow and carefully placing them into her basket. "Hhhhh," the little girl gasped, nearly dropping her basket. A large werewolf approached her, standing as a man stands, and breathing heavily over her. He held in his hand the document written in blood, and presented it in the face of the little girl and angrily stated to her, "You cannot pick these flowers. You have no legal right to be here. See I am in charge around here now; you are not. You have come to the age to fulfil the agreement written by your ancestors with me."

The little girl shook, but her small hands were still able to hold the basket of flowers she had collected. "I am only a child, a little girl, what have I done to deserve this?" she asked as she quivered.

"You will come with me," stated the werewolf, growling at her. He then snatched her by the wrist to take her to his castle. Her basket of fresh flowers fell to the ground, tears ran from her eyes and down her cheeks. She fought and hit, she even kicked the werewolf. She screamed, but nothing stopped him!

He dragged her into his castle; she was helpless, hopeless. His castle was filled with werewolves just like him, vampires, and other blood thirsty creatures.

"What am I to do?" the little girl cried. Her cheeks were no longer rosy; they had now taken on a grey appearance.

"You will obey me. I am in charge of your time and seasons from now on" he snarled at her.

"So, there's no point in trying then? Or being hopeful?" she bravely questioned the werewolf, even though she was broken and distraught inside.

"That's right, from now on you do what I say. And if you do escape outside my walls, I will find you and I will destroy everything you touch."

Jennifer was horrified at what this little girl was experiencing. "Can you see this, Holy Spirit? This is not right and it's not fair! This is not right or fair at all! This little girl is paying the price for what someone else did in her family line. She is paying the price for a blood oath that she did not make! It's not fair!" Jennifer protested to Holy Spirit.

"*What will you do for this little girl Jenni?*" Holy Spirit tested her. "I'm going to get justice for her! This is not right and it is not fair! I'm going to call on Him and use His Justice system... now!" she answered with a righteous anger bubbling up from her inner most being. Jennifer was determined to get freedom for the little girl from the only One she knew could release her from this entrapment — instantly and permanently!

The Redemption

Jennifer immediately called upon the name of the LORD. "Where are You Jesus?!"

"*I am here Jenni, right beside you,*" He answered.

Jennifer looked at Jesus. "This is not right LORD!" she cried with righteous anger, pointing at the scene of the little girl picking flowers, just as the werewolf approached. Jesus smiled and gently took Jennifer's right hand between His. Jennifer looked at their joined hands, wondering how this could possibly help the little girl. She looked up at Him to start asking more questions.

But as she did, she noticed that their joined hands overlaid the scenario... Jennifer and Jesus, were now superimposed over the vision of the little girl picking flowers as the werewolf approached. It was like He had paused the vision and somehow brought Jennifer to line 'a.' The line that the Holy Spirit had taught her about when Jesus rescues someone from the enemy's plan on line 'b' and makes it 'ab initio' — as if it never existed!

"Where are we LORD?" Jennifer enquired, wanting to know if her heart was correct. Had she been supernaturally transposed by His Justice, and was she experiencing it in the Heavenly realm as it was all about to unfold?

"*We are here.*" Jesus answered folding His hands and placing them gently upon His gold sash that rested near His waist.

"Where is 'here' LORD?" she requested again, thinking that perhaps He did not understand her question. Jesus smiled at her and replied, "*Jenni, we are in Me.*"

"Oh... oh," she whispered, astonished with what He had just revealed to her. Jesus then reminded her heart of the scripture from John chapter 1 that Holy Spirit had shared with her when she first stood on the sixteenth step. Jennifer quietly started to recite some of the scripture as she processed what was happening. "All things were made through Him... nothing is made without Him... in Him is life... His life is light... darkness can't overcome it."

Jesus looked intently at Jennifer, "*So why are we here Jenni?*" She closed her eyes and pondered who He is.

Jesus re-tucked her thick, shiny, smooth hair behind her ears as He waited for her heart to catch up and respond to Him. Then, her heart released the words she needed and she replied, "Because You are the Creator with Father

God. You are life, You are light and You are Justice."

"So, what are you wanting Me to do for you then Jenni?" Jesus enquired, as He stirred the area of her heart that had been robbed by the blood oath taken out by her ancestors.

She began to feel His anointing flow over her as tears of compassion ran down her cheeks. Jennifer then presented her request to her KING. "I'm asking for justice, Your Justice, for the pain this little girl experienced. The pain that created wounds, bruises, callouses and chastisement. Because she didn't know to ask You to give her Your Justice for the pain that had been travelling down her family line — my family line, affecting me and my offspring…"

"Go on," He urged her.

"… I'm asking You to forgive my ancestors who sold out the women in my family line to gain ungodly power, wealth and influence, which robbed the women of the gifts You gave them," she continued. "I'm asking for You to restore sevenfold what has been stolen, according to Your Word in Proverbs 6:31: 'Yet when he is found, he must restore sevenfold; he may have to give up all the substance of his house.' I'm asking you to return to the women in our family line Your initial blessing," she stated, laying out her case before the LORD.

"The scripture in Genesis 1:28: 'Then God blessed them, and God said to them, be fruitful and multiply, fill the earth and subdue it…' I'm asking You for Your Justice, to restore this to the women in my family line so they will 'be fruitful, multiply, fill the earth, and subdue it.' At present they are being robbed! Their times and seasons are affected, their fruits are being eaten, they are being subdued by this inherited oath, and they cannot fill the earth and **subdue it** because of it! I'm asking You for Your Justice LORD, in Jesus name," she added as fast as she could, desiring Him to give her what His Word said she could have, what the women in her family line could have. What the little girl in the vision could have!

Jesus smiled at Jennifer and rubbed her cheek with His right thumb. *"I will give her justice Jenni, My Justice. I will see to it that she receives it swiftly. I will restore to you and the women in your family line the gifts and years the locusts have stolen sevenfold. I will restore to you and the women in your family line the rulership of the times and seasons."*

Tears continued to run down Jennifer's cheeks; but now they were tears of joy!

"Thank You LORD, thank You for Your mercy and grace toward me and all of the woman who have gone before me, and those who will come after me in my family line. Thank You for Your love, Your goodness, Your wisdom, Your faithfulness," she cried as she pressed herself against His body to squeeze Him as tightly as she could.

"LORD, where are Your scars? I felt them before… many times, but now they are gone?" Jennifer questioned Him as she pulled away from their embrace to look intently at His face for His answer.

"It's ok Jenni, do not be afraid, only believe. My scars are tangible to My Beloved to clearly show them "it is finished," that they are healed, that everything has been dealt with. It increases their faith and ability to build in their hearts when they touch them. And it helps them to understand and know that I have paid the full price for their freedom — that My Justice, Peace and Purpose is given without cost," He explained as He smoothed the hair on her forehead.

Jennifer's Mountain

Jennifer's eyes lit up as never before. She scanned the atmosphere around her to find that she was sitting on the throne of gold on top of her mountain. Her surroundings were now made of green pastures, blooming with flowers that swayed in the wind of the Spirit. The river of life swirled around her mountain from her throne down to the bottom and through the gate where children ran and played. Jennifer found a golden crown resting upon her head as she went to run her fingers through her thick, dark wavy hair. "Jesus, I can't wear this — You are the KING, You have done all of this" she stated as she swept her right hand over the vastness of the area.

"Jenni, you do not understand, you created all of this with our Father, Myself, and Holy Spirit before the beginning of time and agreed to rule and reign here when we reasoned together. Now it is My pleasure to give you this seat and crown to symbolise to the Heavens and the earth, that you are a king and priest with Me," He explained to her, touching the crown on her head.

"Thank You LORD. How will I ever repay You?" she asked.

"You can't" He replied with a chuckle. *"All of this is My gift to you. All I require of you is that you be who We created you to be and enjoy doing it. So go for it. Create, build, transform the hearts of mankind — be My assistant. Most importantly, enjoy Me, enjoy being you, and enjoy those around you to enable My Kingdom to expand on the earth."*

"So… live a life of 'shama' then. Listen and follow Holy Spirit and bring glory to Father God's name," Jennifer replied confidently. She then realised that she now had the capacity to fulfil His invitation successfully. She would speak words of life into people. The world would know she was sent, because she had what she needed to glorify His name — His Kingdom and His love within her heart.

Jennifer had allowed Him to make her, to bless her, to make her name great through His Justice, His Peace and His Purpose… so she could be a blessing to all those upon the earth.

♥

Psalm 24:1-7

The earth is the LORD's, and all its fullness,
the world and those who dwell therein.
For He has founded it upon the seas,
and established it upon the waters.

Who may ascend into the hill of the LORD?
And who may stand in His holy place?
He who has clean hands and a pure heart,
who has not lifted up his soul to an idol,
nor sworn deceitfully.
He shall receive blessing from the LORD,
and righteousness from the God of his salvation.
This is Jacob, the generation of those who seek him,
who seek Your face. Selah

Lift up your heads, O you gates!
And be lifted up, you everlasting doors!
And the King of glory shall come in.

Appendix

"Let it be it known to the king that the Jews who came up from you to us **have come to us at Jerusalem, and are rebuilding the rebellious and evil city, and are finishing its walls and repairing the foundations.**"
Ezra 4:12

"And now for **a little while grace has been shown from the LORD our God,** to leave us a remnant to escape, and **to give us a peg in His holy place, that our God may enlighten our eyes and give us a measure of revival** in our bondage."
Ezra 9:8

"In whom the **whole building, being fitted together, grows into a holy temple in the Lord, in whom you also are being built together for a dwelling place of God in the Spirit.**"
Ephesians 2:21-22

"I will fasten him as a peg in a **secure place**, and he will become a glorious throne to his father's house. They will hang on him **all the glory of his father's house, the offspring and the posterity, all vessels of small quantity, from the cups to all the pitchers.**"
Isaiah 22:23-24

"But in a great house there are not only vessels of gold and silver, but also of wood and clay, some for honor and some for dishonor. Therefore if anyone **cleanses himself from the later, he will be a vessel for honor, sanctified and useful for the Master, prepared for every good work.**"
2 Timothy 2:20-21

*"Father; I step through the veil in faith and trust. I cover
my life under the testimony of the Blood of Jesus…"*

Step One
[1]Matthew 22:37-40
[2]Isaiah 61:8
[3]Psalm 19:12-14

Step Two
[4]Isaiah 1:18
[5]Psalm 34:8
[6]Proverbs 8:12-14

Step Three
[7]Matthew 8:12
[8]2 Timothy 2:19
[9]John 15:5
[10]Jeremiah 6:16

Step Four
[11]Psalm 119:76
[12]Psalm 23:5

Step Five
[13]Deuteronomy 28:13
[14]Deuteronomy 11:18
[15]Matthew 22:37-38
[16]Psalm 84:11

Step Six
[17]Psalm 37:5
[18]Matthew 7:24-25
[19]Proverbs 4:23

Step Seven
[20]Song of Solomon 4:3
[21]Psalm 105:19

Step Eight
[22]Hebrews 12:2
[23]Matthew 7:1-3
[24]Matthew 6:33-34

Step Nine
[25]John 3:16

Step Ten
[26]Luke 24:49
[27]Isaiah 58:9

Step Eleven
[28]John 16:8

Step Twelve
[29]John 10:10
[30]Matthew 5:16

Step Thirteen
[31]Luke 17:20b-21
[32]Jeremiah 1:10

Step Fourteen
[33]Psalm 125:1-2
[34]Joel 2:12-13
[35]Isaiah 41:10
[36]Proverbs 25:12

Step Fifteen
[37]Romans 11:36
[38]Psalm 91:12-16
[39]Revelation 5:10

Step Sixteen
[40]John 1:1-5
[41]John 6:68-69